CW01622448

THE DOCTOR'S CHANCE AT FOREVER

ALISON ROBERTS

Boldwood

First published in 2012 as *The Legendary Playboy Surgeon*. This edition published in Great Britain in 2026 by Boldwood Books Ltd.

Cover Design by Head Design Ltd.

Cover Images: Shutterstock

A CIP catalogue record for this book is available from the British Library.

Paperback ISBN 978-1-80600-794-3

Large Print ISBN 978-1-80600-793-6

Hardback ISBN 978-1-80600-792-9

Trade Paperback ISBN 978-1-80656-402-6

Ebook ISBN 978-1-80600-795-0

Kindle ISBN 978-1-80600-796-7

Audio CD ISBN 978-1-80600-787-5

MP3 CD ISBN 978-1-80600-788-2

Digital audio download ISBN 978-1-80600-790-5

This book is printed on certified sustainable paper. Boldwood Books is dedicated to putting sustainability at the heart of our business. For more information please visit https://www.boldwoodbooks.com/about-us/sustainability/

Boldwood Books Ltd, 23 Bowerdean Street, London, SW6 3TN

www.boldwoodbooks.com

1

What on earth was going on here?

As she stepped out of the lift, Dr Kate Graham found herself staring at the expanse of linoleum lining the floor of this hospital corridor. The flecked beige was clearly marked by... tyre tracks?

Very odd.

Not that a lot of hospital equipment didn't have wheels, and it was conceivable that a particularly heavy item – a portable X-ray machine, for example – might have pneumatic tyres on its wheels, but these marks suggested the kind of wheels that belonged to something that needed a roadway to get from A to B.

The track marks were leading towards the children's ward, which was also Kate's intended destination, but she would probably have followed them anyway. Any distraction from what was waiting for her down in the bowels of St Patrick's hospital was welcome. Something that seemed highly inappropriate and might need sorting out was even better. Kate could potentially defuse the horrible tension that had been building in her for some time now by directing it elsewhere.

Good grief...!

Kate could see what had left the wheel marks as soon as she rounded a corner. A gleaming, bright red monstrosity at the end of the corridor, just outside the double doors that she knew led to the wide playroom, which was a space enjoyed by any child deemed well enough. Whatever idiot had thought it might be okay to bring a *motorbike*, for heaven's sake, right into a ward full of seriously sick children?

The playroom was well past the nurses' station where Kate had been headed to collect some urgent samples for the pathology department, but she didn't even slow down as she passed the doorway. Not that the area was attended at the moment, anyway, because staff members and patients alike were crowded around the astonishing spectacle of the motorbike and the leather-clad figure beside it, who was at that moment lifting a helmet from his head.

Connor Matthews.

Well, no surprises there. The orthopaedic surgeon who specialised in child cancer cases might be something of a legend here at St Pat's, but he failed to impress Kate. He was... *disreputable*, that's what he was. He might fit in just fine when he was in an operating theatre, but when that hat and mask came off he looked, quite frankly, unprofessional. He was weeks behind a much-needed haircut for those shaggy black curls and at least several days behind basic personal grooming such as shaving. If he wasn't in scrubs, his appearance was even worse. Jeans with badly frayed hems. Black T-shirts under a leather jacket. *Cowboy* boots! Worse than his physical appearance, though, Connor Matthews broke rules.

All sorts of rules, and many of them were far less superficial than a dress code. He was renowned for not following established protocols and he seemed to enjoy being in places he wasn't supposed to be. Good grief, last week he'd not only delivered a pathology sample to her department in person, in order to queue-jump, he'd also hung around and peered through microscopes himself until a diagnosis had been made. If she'd been in the laboratory when he'd turned up, he wouldn't have got away with it just by flashing that admittedly charming smile.

Was that how he'd engineered the appalling demonstration of rule-flouting that was going on here now? The paediatric nursing staff had probably melted under the onslaught of his careless charm, the way the lab technicians had last week. They were certainly bedazzled right now. Nobody had noticed Kate's arrival and they weren't making room for her to get any closer to the centre of attention. Everybody was riveted by what was happening in front of them.

Connor Matthews was not a small man. As he sank to his haunches in front of a small pyjama-clad boy, the leather of his pants strained across muscular thighs and the rivets on the back of the biker's jacket were put under considerable stress as it stretched taut across his broad, strong shoulders. Kate could almost hear a collective, wistful sigh from all the women present.

Connor was oblivious to her glare, of course. He had the motorbike helmet cradled in hands that looked too big to be capable of the delicate skills she knew he displayed in Theatre. She'd also heard how good he was with children too, and that was more believable, given the way he was talking quietly to the boy as though they were the only two people in existence. And then he eased the oversized helmet onto the boy's head, got to his feet and lifted the child onto the seat of the motorbike with a movement that was careful enough not to compromise a tangle of IV lines and gentle enough to elicit an audible sigh from the women this time. The boy's mother was holding the IV pole steady with one hand. She was pressing the fingertips of her other hand to her face to try and stem her tears as Connor showed the boy how to hold the controls.

And then he did the unthinkable. He reached out, turned a key and pushed a button, and the engine of the motorbike roared into life, emitting a puff of black smoke from the wide, shiny silver exhaust pipe. There were children in here suffering from major respiratory illnesses, for heaven's sake. Asthma, cystic fibrosis, compromised immune systems and... and everybody around her was smiling and clapping. One of the nurses was taking photographs. Kate stood, rigid with indignation as the show broke up shortly thereafter. The engine of the motorbike was switched off. The small boy relinquished the helmet and was gathered up by his mother and taken away. Staff members remembered urgent tasks and dispersed in different directions, and the other children were wheeled, led or carried back to where they were supposed to be, many of them craning their necks and sending longing glances back to where the excitement had been happening.

Only Connor remained. He hung the helmet over a handlebar by its chinstrap and kicked the stand up. With a movement that made the heavy machine look weightless, he turned it and began to wheel it back down the corridor, leaving a new set of track marks on the floor. The young girl with a mop and bucket and the uniform of the cleaning staff merely smiled shyly as he went past, ducking her head with pleasure as he made some apologetic comment about the mess. He looked up then in the direction he was travelling and that was when he saw Kate. A curiously guarded expression came over his features as he closed the distance between them.

* * *

Busted!

By no less than Princess Prim and Proper from Pathology. The alliteration was pleasing enough to tease a quirk out of his lips, but Connor wasn't about to allow a real smile to form. Partly because he knew he could be in for some serious flak if some of the rule-makers around here heard about this morning's stunt, but it was more because he was facing someone who clearly didn't have the compassion to have been as moved by what had just occurred as everyone else was.

The lump in his own throat was only just beginning to melt now and it was being replaced by another kind of constriction. One that had its roots in much darker emotions. The kind he'd grown up with. Feelings of sadness and frustration and... failure.

Attack might be the best form of defence.

Connor smiled. Always a good diversionary tactic. He raised his eyebrows as well, to suggest a pleasant surprise.

'Kate, isn't it? Fancy meeting you here.'

The subtext wasn't very subtle. This was his patch. With the kids that deserved all the help they could get and their families who needed it just as desperately. This woman with her palpable air of disapproval belonged in the basement of St Pat's. Along with her test tubes and microscopes and the bodies of those unfortunate enough not to make it out of hospital.

She didn't smile back. No surprises there.

'Not everyone delivers urgent samples to the pathology department in person,' she said.

Her subtext wasn't exactly subtle either. Connor met her glare steadily.

'Sometimes,' he said, choosing his words carefully, 'you find yourself in a situation that requires a bit of lateral thinking. Going the proverbial extra mile, if you like.'

His gaze travelled slowly over Kate. Her hair was glossy and black and had the potential to be attractive, but it was scraped back into the tightest ponytail ever with its length braided into a very solid-looking rope. Her eyelashes were visible, despite the thick rims of her glasses, and they were also thick and black. God given, no doubt, because Connor couldn't see any evidence of make-up being applied.

There were sensible, flat shoes on the other end of her body and, in between, he could see a small amount of a plain, straight skirt. She wore a white coat, for heaven's sake. Who did that these days? And even the people who felt the need to advertise some kind of clinical status would never, ever be uncool enough to button it up like that.

When he lifted his gaze to her face again, he found Kate staring back at him as if he was speaking a foreign language. He suppressed a sigh.

'No, I don't suppose you would ever feel like doing that, would you?'

'If you mean I wouldn't feel like bringing a motorbike indoors and puffing poisonous exhaust fumes around a whole lot of sick children, you'd be right. I can't believe that you thought it was—'

Her outraged admonition was interrupted by someone hurrying towards them.

It was the mother of the little boy from the back of the bike. She'd courageously managed to hold back her tears earlier, but they were flowing freely now.

'Thank you,' she said, her words choked.

'Hey...' Connor held the weight of the bike with one hand, using his other arm to draw the woman close as she wrapped her arms around his neck. 'It was nothing, Jeannie.'

Jeannie gave an enormous sniff. 'I have to get back. It... it won't be long now.'

'I know.' The lump was back in Connor's throat. He needed to find a space by himself for a few minutes. Preferably with a bit of speed involved. Maybe he'd take the bike for a quick spin on the motorway.

Jeannie stood still for a moment, taking a huge gulp of air to steady herself. 'I just had to say thank you,' she whispered. 'Liam... went to sleep with the biggest smile on his face.'

'I'm glad.'

'I don't think he was even aware of any pain when he was sitting on your bike. The photos are... are...'

'Something you'll treasure.' Connor had to swallow hard. 'Go and be with Liam, Jeannie. He needs his mum.'

Her face crumpled again as she turned away. Connor had to take a very deep, slow breath because he was suddenly aware that Kate was still there and that she'd heard every word of that emotional exchange. Surely she couldn't have missed the undercurrent? The reason why Connor had been prepared to break so many rules here?

She hadn't. He could see it in her face, which had gone a shade paler. And in the way her eyes seemed to have grown a lot bigger. He hadn't noticed how blue they were before.

'I... I don't know what to say,' she stammered awkwardly.

'Don't say anything, then,' Connor advised wearily. He had to get away. If he was going to cry, it had to be out on the motorway where the moisture could be attributed to the wind getting in his eyes.

He got the motorbike moving again with a jerk. Kate was still standing there, opening and closing her mouth as though she really wanted to say something but couldn't think what. She looked like a stranded fish.

And she was still giving off a disapproving vibe. Maybe she still intended to do something about his misdemeanour. Connor felt sandwiched between the constraints of the establishment she represented, with its inability to do enough for someone like Liam, and the weight of grief he could feel emanating from that private room down the end of the ward where a mother would be cradling her dying child.

He had to push back against one of those barriers or he wouldn't be able to breathe.

'You know what?' Connor shook his head. 'You need to get a life. You're about as buttoned up as that ridiculous coat you're wearing.'

* * *

Her coat?

What was wrong with her coat?

Kate collected the samples that needed urgent testing to see whether a two-year-old girl had meningitis. The nurse who handed them over had clearly been crying very recently. Other staff members were huddled at the central station, clutching handfuls of tissues. One took a sheet of paper emerging from the printer in the corner and held it up.

Someone else stifled a sob.

Kate craned her neck a little to see what they were looking at. It was a large copy of a photograph. A small boy, his head almost obscured by the oversized helmet he was wearing so that what jumped out at the viewer was his grin. And what a grin. Bright enough to make anything else in the image irrelevant, even the tangle of IV lines that were coming from the central line just under his collar bone.

She turned and walked away with something close to panic nipping at her heels. The emotions were so raw here, but what was she hurrying towards? Something even worse?

Arriving at the pathology department, Kate delivered the samples. 'Do them immediately,' she instructed. 'Phone through the results but make sure a hard copy goes straight to the ward.'

She eyed an empty slot at the bench. 'Maybe I should do it myself.'

'They're waiting for you downstairs.' The lab technician's grimace conveyed sympathy. They all knew what was waiting for Kate this afternoon. What they didn't know was how unbearably difficult it was going to be.

* * *

'I don't think I can do it.'

The head of the pathology department, Lewis Blackman, said nothing for a moment. He gestured for Kate to sit down in the small, windowless office.

In his early sixties, Lewis was a quiet man. Overweight, silver-haired and thoughtful.

'Remind me why you chose pathology as a specialty, Kate?' Oh... Lord... was he going to tell her she wasn't suitable? Everybody expected her to take over as HoD when Lewis retired in a few years. She expected it herself but how could she if she couldn't handle the downside of what this job entailed?

Lewis was waiting patiently for a response. Kate's thoughts travelled back in time. To when she'd been a nurse and had hated the frustration of being on the sidelines. Being treated as a lesser being by those who got to make the diagnoses and then treat the patients. She thought of how hard she'd struggled to support herself by doing killer night shifts while she'd put herself through medical school. Then she remembered what it had been like being a junior doctor. She'd probably had more respect than others, being a little older and more experienced in the world of medicine, but she'd still felt as though she was on the outside somehow.

'I saw pathology as being the lynchpin in almost every critical case,' she said. 'No doctor, no matter how skilled they are, can do their job to the best of their ability unless they know exactly what they're dealing with. Sometimes they're holding their breath for what we can tell them, like when they're in Theatre, waiting for the result of a tumour analysis.'

Unbidden, her thoughts flashed up an image of Connor Matthews. Not in Theatre, with his scalpel poised waiting for word from the pathology department, though. Oh, no, she could picture him dressed in his leathers. Dark and disreputable and prepared to break any rule in the book to grant a wish for a dying child.

She sucked in a slightly ragged breath.

Lewis was nodding. 'True enough. But you could stay in a laboratory to do all that. You could avoid being anywhere near the morgue and you'd never have to do an autopsy.'

Kate's heart took a dive. 'But that can be the most exciting part of this job. Finding out what went wrong... so... so it doesn't happen again. It can be like putting together the most challenging jigsaw puzzle in the world. Finding the piece that maybe nobody even knew was missing.'

Lewis smiled, nodding. 'Satisfying, isn't it?' He eyed Kate. 'You do the neatest, most thorough autopsies I've ever seen, and

I'm including my own. You could have been a brilliant surgeon, you know.'

'I'm happy where I am. I have my life exactly the way I want it.'

Lewis merely lifted an eyebrow. What was he thinking? That she was thirty-five years old and single? That she lived alone and had a passion for things in test tubes or on microscope slides or, worse, for dead bodies? That she was a freak? Someone to be pitied?

'You need challenges, though, don't you? Something to keep that sharp mind of yours intrigued? Isn't that why you want to take over the forensic specialty?'

Kate had to nod but her teeth were worrying away at her bottom lip as she did so.

'Coroners' cases are often about an unexplained death that has a medical cause or trauma that's come from an accident, but some of the most important cases are crime related and the detail we can give can make a difference to whether the perpetrator of a crime is punished. Our report can be essential for making sure a murderer or rapist or child abuser can't do any more harm out there.'

Kate was still nodding. She knew that. She had also had a taste of the kind of excitement that came from unravelling the totally unexpected. Of not knowing what could come through the door, disguised in the heavy latex of a body bag. Sometimes the victims came directly from the scene of the crime. Often, though, they made it to hospital and lived for a short time. Occasionally, there was the added trauma of someone having to make the decision to turn off life support. Like today's case.

Lewis was looking somewhere over the top of Kate's head now. 'You're a clever woman, Kate. Do you know, it took me over a year to realise that you were actively avoiding any case that involved young children? You always had such a good reason for not being available, but eventually I began to see the pattern and when you took the first sick day I'd ever known you to have, I understood what was going on. At least, I understood *what*. I have no idea *why*.'

He paused for moment as he met her gaze. 'Is it something you want to talk about?'

Kate shook her head. Lewis nodded his, slowly, as if he hadn't expected any other response.

'The most vulnerable people out there are children,' he said quietly. 'Especially babies. It breaks my heart to have to deal with them in there.' His hand waved in the direction of the adjacent morgue with its stainless-steel benches and buckets and the grim tools of this part of their trade.

'But someone has to,' Lewis continued. 'And whether it's medical or forensic, it has to be done. I've given you as long as I can to get used to the idea. I can be with you today if it would help, but this has to be make or break, Kate. If it's something you can't face then now's the time to decide. If you can't, that's absolutely fine, but we'll have to rethink the direction your career is taking.'

She'd known it was coming. She'd been stepping closer to the edge of the precipice for a long time. She had steeled herself for this day and she'd thought she was ready. Right up until she'd seen that desperate sadness in the depths of Connor Matthew's already dark eyes. Until she'd felt the touch of emotions so painful they were impossible to block completely.

But if she stepped back from the edge, where would she go?

She would be trapped in a prison of her own making. Lewis was right. She had to have challenge. Something that gave real meaning to her life. Kate could almost feel the frustration now. See herself circling some vast laboratory, hemmed in by test tubes and specimen jars and thin glass slides. Ranks and ranks of them that looked like prison bars all of a sudden.

'I'll do it,' she whispered.

'Want me to stay?'

Kate raised her gaze to meet the concern in Lewis's eyes directly. He was offering her a lifeline. A rope so that she could abseil down the precipice instead of stepping into the void alone.

'Thanks, but I think it's best if I do it by myself.'

* * *

She did do it.

By herself.

Hours later, Kate was driving herself home and she had never been so exhausted. Physically and emotionally. Her head was still full of it. The procrastination before she'd entered the morgue. Reading the clinical notes on Peyton, the week-old baby girl who was waiting for her.

The cerebral scan demonstrates no apparent blood flow, indicative of brain death. While there could have been some residual brain-stem function and life could have been prolonged with mechanical ventilation, there would have been no recovery...

That wobble in her voice when she'd started her dictation.

...a full-term infant with no apparent external abnormalities...

The microscopic appearance of the slides made from tiny slivers of brain tissue.

The ends of the axons show shortening consistent with having been sheared off by violent shaking or rotational injury.

Clinical notes or dictation that had the undercurrent of such draining emotional involvement. Peyton's mother was only seventeen and she'd hidden the pregnancy for as long as she could. Long enough to take termination out of the equation as a possibility. She lived with a large dysfunctional extended family and nobody was talking now. Who had shaken this tiny baby and caused the fatal injuries? What kind of unbearable stress had been going on? It was so easy to judge in cases like this, but Kate knew, more than most people, the damage that stress could cause.

She didn't want to think about it. Not on a personal level. Because if she did, she would remember the pain of losing a tiny person that she could have loved so much. That could have loved *her*.

She didn't have to think about it. She was heading towards her sanctuary. Her beautiful home where she could play the music she loved and cook the food that she was so good at creating, and she could even have a glass of wine tonight because she'd certainly earned it. She could soak in the peace and comfort of the world she'd created, and it would heal her soul because she would be able to tap into the strength she knew she had.

Kate turned down the long driveway, overhung by the huge oak trees that made a leafy tunnel in summer. Her lovely old house nestled at the end of the driveway with its antique lion's head knocker on the heavy wooden front door. There were brick steps leading from the crushed shell pathway and...

And on the top of the steps, something large and human that launched itself towards Kate as she rounded the corner of the house from the garage.

'Kate! Oh... thank God... I've been waiting for you for *ever*.'

2

'*Bella*! What on earth are you doing here?'

Kate's initial shock gave way to a mix of joy and dread. She knew her niece too well and she had just spotted the suitcase near her door. What was Bella running away from?

'I tried to ring but you didn't pick up and then I thought, why don't I just surprise you?' Sheer happiness bubbled from Bella in the form of laughter. 'Are you surprised?'

'Oh... yeah...' The tight hug Kate had been locked in was loosened enough for her to step back a little. Good grief... Bella had become even more gorgeous in the months since she'd last seen her. Her hair was much longer. A tumble of shiny blonde waves. Legs that looked like they went on forever, thanks to the super-short mini-skirt and the high, high heels.

It was impossible not to smile back. 'It's been way too long, Bells. We've got some catching up to do.'

'Well, we've got all the time in the world.' Bella laughed and lunged for her suitcase. 'Let's go inside. Aren't you going to ask me what I'm doing here?'

'I already did.' Kate fished for her key, shaking her head. It was spinning now. The plan to banish any lingering aftermath of her day's work in peaceful solitude was blown away.

The world was a different place when Annabelle Graham was around.

Kate's front door opened into an elegant panelled hallway with a Persian runner adding warm crimson tones to all the dark woodwork. Like the rest of her home, the hallway was furnished with carefully chosen, beautiful antique furniture and ornaments, everything in exactly the right place and without a speck of dust to mar gleaming surfaces.

Bella's case was missing a wheel. It bumped and swayed along the runner, bunching up the worn areas on the priceless carpet. Bella was just as out of sync with her surroundings but it didn't bother her in the slightest.

'Oh... look... you've still got that collection of old keys! Aren't they gorgeous? D'you remember when you found the first one? In that junk shop you were hiding in when you ran away?'

'I didn't run away. I'd just gone for a walk.'

Bella gave her the same smile she had when she'd discovered Kate in that junk shop all those years ago. The one that said she understood and it was okay. Kate had never forgotten it. How could she? The bond between these two women had been forged right then, even though Bella had only been six years old at the time.

And maybe that smile was exactly what Kate needed right now. How could solitude and tapping into an inner strength, even in perfect surroundings, compete with that kind of acceptance and unconditional love? Even if Bella had never known, and hopefully never would know, the whole story, this feeling of not being so alone in the world was a precious thing.

So Kate simply smiled back. 'I've missed you, Bells.'

'Oh... me, too.' Bella abandoned her overstuffed bag in favour of giving her aunt another tight hug. 'And I've got so much to tell you.' She swung away again, as light on her feet as a dancer. 'Am I in this room again?'

The light was flicked on in a butter-yellow room that had a bay window and an antique brass bedstead with a patchwork quilt.

'Of course. It's the only guest room with an en suite. How long are you staying?'

But Bella had opened her case and the contents seemed to explode in relief.

'I've got something in here for you. Oh... where is it?'

Scraps of lacy underwear like nothing Kate had ever worn were tossed aside. Long black boots with heels that could double as lethal weapons followed. A battered teddy bear was snatched up, cuddled and then deposited tenderly on the bed to nestle between snowy-white, frilled pillowcases.

'Oh, my goodness... you *still* have that bear?'

'Are you kidding? You gave him to me. I couldn't sleep without Red Ted.'

Within the space of sixty seconds the room looked like a bomb site, with clothing, cosmetics and even books strewn about. And then Bella triumphantly held up a small package, exquisitely wrapped in primrose-yellow tissue paper, with a ribbon that matched the tiny bouquet of dried wild flowers it held in place.

Kate's chest felt tight as she accepted the gift. This was pure Bella. Disorganised, irresponsible and unbelievably messy, but amongst the chaos were moments that were simply perfect. The kind you stored in your memory bank for when you needed to remember that life was worth living.

'Go on, open it, Kate.' Bella was hugging herself with excitement.

Inside the lovingly wrapped package was a photograph in a beaten, silver frame. A small girl and a young woman sitting together on a swing seat, their arms around each other. They weren't looking at the camera because they were smiling at each other.

'D'you remember this? I found it in an old album and Dad said I could have it copied and framed.'

'Oh...' The tight feeling in Kate's chest was making it difficult to draw in a breath. Her smile felt wobbly. 'How old were you then?'

'Dunno. Eight or nine? That tree blew down in a storm last year, did Dad tell you?'

'No. That's sad.'

Bella shrugged. 'It was getting too big, anyway. It blocked half our sun. What is it with you and Dad and trees? You're practically buried in a forest here. Doesn't it feel like you're walled off from the world or something?'

Kate mirrored the shrug. Maybe the world was walled off from her and that was the way she liked it.

'It's a gorgeous photo. Thank you. You shouldn't be spending your money on me, though. I thought you were saving up to go overseas.'

'I am. That's why I'm here. Nurses get paid better in the big smoke.' Bella did a little twirl. 'I've got a job at St Pat's. How cool is that?'

Kate's jaw dropped. 'A job?'

'Yep. Not where I want to be to start with, mind you. I have to do a three-month rotation in Theatre and then in Geriatrics.' Bella grimaced. 'But if I can stand it, I get to be in my favourite place after that. With all the babies in Paeds.'

'So this is a permanent position?'

Bella laughed. 'Permanent? Me? Are you kidding? No. I just want to save enough to get offshore. A year, or maybe six months if I save hard.'

She grinned. 'And if my lovely, kind auntie will let me live with her.'

Kate still hadn't closed her mouth. The whirlwind that was Bella was a joy in small doses, but for the next six months to a year? Could she cope? Her head was still spinning. No, her whole world seemed to be spinning. Bella was the flip side of her own personality. Impulsive where she was cautious. Ready to drop anything for a better offer where Kate hated to change routines. Prepared to take risks to shake the maximum amount of joy out of life where Kate retreated to safety every time.

Inexplicably, the image of Connor Matthews came to mind. As if he was in the room with them, watching her. Comparing her with Kate. Nodding, as if to say, *Yeah... here's a woman who has a life.*

'Can I stay? Please, please, please?'

'Of... course you can.'

'I won't be any trouble, honest. I'll help with the cooking and cleaning and everything. And I'll probably be out heaps. You won't even notice I'm here.'

Kate's gaze took in the wild array of possessions scattered around the guest bedroom. She knew exactly what the kitchen would look like if Bella took a turn at cooking. Yes, she'd go out a lot because her niece was never without friends for long, but she'd be coming in at 2 or 3 a.m. Or not coming in at all and she would be left lying awake wondering where Bella was and whether she was safe. Yes, there were times when there was a definite downside of the vicarious living that could be done by being around Bella, but there was also an attraction. A buzz. Life became much more colourful. Fun.

She couldn't banish that image of Connor from her head. She could imagine him smiling now. Approvingly but with an edge of smugness.

A smile that said, *Watch and learn, Dr Graham.*

Birds of a feather, her niece and the maverick surgeon? No. Bella didn't set out to break rules. She either didn't notice they were there or thought she could get away with anything by using a combination of contrition and charm. And it usually worked. If it didn't, she sucked up any punishment because she had brought it on herself. Which was probably why she was unrepentant about the broken hearts she'd been leaving in her wake for years now. Dating was a game that had to be played according to Bella's rules, and she was always upfront about her plans for her future. She wasn't going to consider a permanent relationship until she was thirty and then she was going to choose the perfect man and settle down to have a dozen kids.

Another facet of the flip side. Watching Bella grow up was the closest Kate would ever get to having a child of her own.

'I'm starving,' Bella announced. 'Ooh... I've got a bottle of wine for you in my handbag. A red. The man in the shop said it was a very good one.'

Kate recognised the label. A nice New Zealand Shiraz. 'Good choice. I've got lamb shanks in the slow cooker. Well done, you.'

Bella laughed. 'Pure luck. I said it came in a bottle so it had to be good.' She held the bottle aloft like a trophy. 'Shall we? You can tell me all about St Pat's while we eat. Like who the hottest doctors are.'

Kate was laughing as she led the way to her kitchen. She could be quite sure that Bella was more than capable of discovering that kind of information for herself in no time at all. In fact, she wouldn't be at all surprised if her niece arrived home on the back of Connor's motorbike within a fortnight.

* * *

The new nurse in Theatre was cute.

Tall and blonde. Blue-eyed and smiley. Just the way Connor Matthews liked his women. The absolute opposite of grim-faced, dark-haired, disapproving females who clearly had no fun in life at all.

So why hadn't he been able to expunge the image of Kate Graham from his mind over the last few days?

Because he felt bad, that's why. It had been a mean thing to say, telling her that she needed to get a life. Adding that her white coat looked ridiculous had been nothing more than childish. And also mean. Connor was not a mean person. The only justification for the way he'd attacked her was that he had been in the middle of a fairly devastating emotional experience.

Connor scrubbed harder at his hands with the soap-impregnated brush. Under his nails. Between his fingers. Hard enough to hurt.

He'd been to young Liam's funeral only yesterday and even during the service he'd been thinking about Kate. A distraction, maybe, from memories that had the potential to wreak havoc in his life even now. He'd thought about the way her face had changed when she'd realised what had actually been going on. The reason he'd done something as outrageous as taking a huge, dirty motorbike into a children's ward. She'd gone so pale. Been so lost for words and... when he'd thought about it later, there'd been something in her eyes that had suggested she was all too familiar with the kind of pain life could dish out sometimes.

How did she know that? What had happened to her?

Something big enough to make her the way she was? As if she didn't want to connect with people. Almost as though she was afraid of the good things life could offer.

Why?

It wasn't as if she was a wimp. It took guts to see a medical degree through. And brain power. And... she wasn't that bad looking. If she undid those buttons and took off those glasses and let her hair do something remotely natural, she could be a different person.

Connor found himself grinning as he angled his reddened but virtually sterile hands under the stream of warm water that he activated with the foot control. He was fantasising about a scene where Kate was the cliché librarian or secretary who loosens her clothing, sheds the spectacles and then shakes out a magnificent mane of hair to transform from a prude into a total vamp for some bemused but appreciative guy.

Like him.

The grin became a grimace. What was he thinking?

Just as well the cute new nurse was there to tie the strings of his gown. She could line up with at least half a dozen of his previous girlfriends and be like a pea in a pod. Great looking and great fun to be with, at least until they got ideas about it meaning more than it did.

This afternoon's case was a long and complicated one. A pillion passenger on his big brother's bike, fourteen-year-old Dillon had such badly broken bones in both his legs and one arm it was going to be a considerable challenge to restore normal function for the teenager. The bones needed precise alignment, using external fixation, and there were tendons and ligaments to patch together. There were also quite long periods when Connor had to step back to allow other specialist surgeons to work their magic with the nerves and blood vessels that needed major repair.

Just the kind of opportunity he knew how to take advantage of. The new nurse was being used as a gofer as she got used to her new working environment and there were times when she wasn't required to fetch or carry anything, so she was standing around watching as well.

Connor stood beside her.

'Hey... you're a new face.'

A bit of a new face anyway, but Connor had seen her disappearing into the female changing room so he'd seen the long blonde hair that was now covered by a disposable hat. The lower half of her face was covered by a mask now too, but he'd already seen her smiling at the nursing staff she'd arrived with. Having only her eyes visible made them even more appealing. Very blue they were. Reminded him of... hell, any number of women probably.

'I'm Bella,' she whispered. 'This is my third day at St Pat's.'

'Connor,' he murmured back. 'Delighted to meet you, Bella.'

Her eyes crinkled at the corners. 'I've heard about you.'

He raised an eyebrow. 'All good things, I hope.'

'Depends on your definition of "good".' Bella giggled and earned a disapproving glance from a senior nurse.

The anaesthetist glanced up with a resigned sigh. 'Give it a rest, Matthews. You're not actually obliged to pick up every new nurse, you know.'

'Hey... I'm just trying to make Bella here feel welcome.'

'Of course you are,' another nurse said. A ripple of laughter went through the theatre staff.

Connor grinned along with them but made a mental note to

point out to his anaesthetist colleague, Mike, that the pot shouldn't be calling the kettle too black. Maybe they'd be able to get a game of squash in this evening and they could discuss it then.

He didn't get another chance to try and chat Bella up. Partly because he was too busy with his work but also because she got sent out of Theatre. Maybe it wasn't really her fault that the accident had happened. Technicians were moving some heavy gear and she got in the way somehow and was almost knocked off her feet. Fortunately, she managed not to fall into the sterile field but nobody was thrilled by the explosive disruption of the heavy metal object she'd been carrying hitting the floor. Bella didn't look too thrilled either, because the collection of used surgical instruments destined for the steriliser had landed on her foot and she was limping quite badly as she slunk out.

She wasn't limping when he spotted her later, having finally escaped the intense surgical session. She was sitting on a couch near a set of lifts, her shoe off, rubbing at her foot.

'Broken bone?' Connor suggested hopefully. 'Do you need the services of an orthopaedic surgeon perhaps?'

Bella scowled at him. 'You don't need to rub it in. I already feel like a complete klutz. It's just a bruise.' She glanced at her mobile phone as a text-message alert sounded. 'Darn... I was hoping to get a ride home but it looks like I'll have to find a bus.'

It was obviously painful to try and put her foot into her shoe. And no wonder; the high heels weren't exactly practical.

Connor couldn't resist a maiden in distress. 'Don't force it,' he advised. 'Leave it off and get some ice on your foot when you get home.'

'That'll be a good look, running for the bus in bare feet.'

'You could call a taxi.' Connor wasn't going to leap to the rescue if it wasn't welcome.

Bella shook her head firmly. 'No way. I'm saving up to head overseas. Every penny counts.'

'In that case, please let me offer to be of service with no scalpel in sight. I have an extra helmet in my locker.'

'Helmet?' Bella's eyes brightened. 'You ride a bike?'

'Sure do.'

Her glance was curious. 'You're an orthopaedic surgeon and you just spent hours putting a teenager back together after he fell off a motorbike. Are you nuts?'

'Probably. Want a ride home?'

Bella grinned. 'Sure.'

* * *

It was all a bit too easy, Connor decided, following Bella's directions to one of the nicer city suburbs. He should be delighted. Here he was, riding his bike with the arms of a beautiful girl wrapped around his waist. A perfect girl, given her liking for motorbikes and the willingness to take a bit of a risk. Taking her home where she'd probably ask him in for a coffee or something and he could offer to check out her foot and one thing would inevitably lead to another and...

There was no challenge here.

The sacrilegious thought that the predictability could be boring was unexpected. Disturbing, even.

So disturbing that Connor suppressed his intention to decline the offer to go inside the rather lovely old house he took her to. He must be tired or something, he decided. Maybe the loss of one of his young patients had affected him more than he'd realised. If an evening with Bella didn't perk him up, he'd know there was something seriously amiss.

'Nice place,' he said, pulling off his helmet.

'It belongs to my aunt,' Bella told him. 'I'm just living with her while I'm working at St Pat's. She works there, too. Come on in. You probably know each other already.'

It was quite possible. Connor was friendly with a lot of the older members of the nursing staff. It was a bonus that Bella wasn't living with a bunch of nurses close to her own age. Even with his current ambivalence about taking this acquaintance any further, it would be rather awkward if an old girlfriend was lurking.

He had time to look around as Bella hobbled up the hallway ahead of him. The house was even nicer on the inside. The aunt clearly had good taste. She could cook, too, judging by the very appetising aroma that was coming from the area Bella veered into at the end of the hallway.

'Oh, my God,' he heard a woman's voice say in concern. 'Why are you limping? What have you done to yourself this time?'

This time? Was Bella accident prone? Maybe she needed looking after.

'Someone moved an X-ray machine in Theatre and I wasn't expecting it,' Bella was explaining as Connor entered the room. 'I lost my grip on this bucket of stuff for the steriliser. It wasn't my fault.'

She twisted her head. 'Was it, Connor?'

But Connor couldn't say anything in Bella's defence. He hadn't seen the incident in the first place and right now it was the furthest thing from his mind. He wasn't even looking at Bella. He was staring at Kate Graham.

At least, he thought it was Kate.

Maybe it was the good twin? This woman looked like Kate but couldn't look more different, which made no sense. His head was spinning. The good twin was wearing jeans. Not just any old jeans. These were beloved old, soft, faded jeans with frayed knees and bare feet beneath them. There was a pale grey T-shirt that was way too big. Big enough for a bare shoulder to be peeping through the neckline. She had no glasses on and her hair hung in a black curtain almost to her waist. A damp kind of curtain, as though she'd just jumped out of a shower.

Or into a movie scene. The prude versus vamp one. To his horror, Connor felt something remarkably like a blush stirring under his skin.

Bella was looking at him and then at Kate. Back and forth as if she was watching a slow-motion tennis game.

'I thought you guys would know each other,' she said. She gave an exasperated huff. 'Kate, this is Connor. I can't remember his last name. He's a surgeon at St Pat's. Connor, this is my aunt, Kate Graham. She hangs out in Pathology.' She shrugged. 'I guess St Pat's is bigger than I thought so maybe your paths never cross.'

Connor was grappling with a very new sensation.

Acute embarrassment? Probably. He couldn't escape the impression that he was seeing something he wasn't supposed to be seeing. As if he was some kind of voyeur peeping through a gap in a curtain. This was even worse than the bit of leftover guilt from the knowledge of how rude he'd been to her the other day. On top of both those unpleasant sensations there was also something he didn't want to identify that had to be blamed on the absurd flight of fancy whilst scrubbing in this afternoon.

He cleared his throat. He had to say something. Kate was doing that totally-lost-for-words thing again.

'They've... um... crossed,' he muttered.

'Oh, good.' Bella gave Kate a quick hug on her way towards the fridge. 'Have we got any ice? I think I should put some on my foot. Connor was kind enough to give me a ride home when I found I couldn't fit my shoe back on.'

'Three days,' Kate muttered, her tone faintly incredulous.

'What?' Bella looked up from the depths of the freezer. 'You think I need to ice my foot for three days?'

'I... No, of course not. If it's still that sore and swollen tomorrow, you'd better get an X-ray. You might have broken something.'

'That's what I thought,' Connor said. 'Heavy things, those buckets. Especially when they're full of the kind of surgical gear we use for rearranging bones.'

Bella had a bag of frozen peas in her hand. 'Can I use these? Much better than ice blocks.'

'Sure. Just don't put them back in the freezer so we eat them by mistake.'

'Speaking of eating...' Bella lifted a lid on a pot. 'Ooh, yum. This smells divine.' She grinned at Connor. 'My aunt is the best cook in the world.'

'I can believe that.' Connor couldn't help licking his lips.

Bella took another look in the pot. 'There's heaps here. Connor could stay and have some dinner with us, couldn't he, Kate?'

* * *

'I... uh...' Kate had no idea what to say.

This was an appalling situation. Nobody from her work had ever been into her home. Her private life was exactly that. Private. She didn't want anyone here. She especially didn't want this man. St Pat's playboy doctor. The one who thought she was buttoned up and needed a life. She had exactly the life she wanted. Private and... and safe.

Until now.

To add insult to injury, she was only just out of the shower and her attire could hardly be deemed presentable. And even if she'd still been in her work clothes she would have felt half-naked with that look he'd given her when he'd come into the room. For heaven's sake, he'd brought Bella home. What did he think he was doing, looking at *her* like that?

And why did it give her the most peculiar ripple of sensation in places she was barely aware of?

She'd known Bella would be capable of discovering the most desirable of any available men at St Pat's, and she had imagined her arriving home on the back of Connor's motorbike. But she'd given it a fortnight. Three days had to be breaking some sort of record, surely? And did she want to sit and watch this embryonic, going-nowhere, purely sexual relationship develop under her gaze? In her own home?

No, she damn well didn't.

Connor was looking just as uncomfortable at the prospect but somehow that didn't mollify Kate in the least.

'I can't stay,' he said hurriedly. 'I've got—'

He didn't get time to finish his sentence because Bella had turned around with the bag of peas in her hand to head for a chair, but when she put weight on her foot, she gave a cry of pain and looked like she was about to fall. Connor stepped forward with commendable speed, caught Bella and practically lifted her bodily onto the kitchen bench.

'That foot needs looking at,' he said firmly. 'Sit still.'

Bella sat.

Connor pulled a kitchen chair close and perched on the

edge of it so that the injured foot was close to eye level. Then he put his hands on it.

'Ouch,' Bella said.

'How much ouch?'

'Lots.'

'You've certainly got a good bruise coming up. Good thing you missed a direct hit on your toes. Can you wiggle them all?'

Bella wiggled.

Kate watched. There was indeed a large bruise on the top of Bella's foot and it probably hurt a great deal. How crazy was it to be feeling... what, envious of her niece right now? No. She was feeling frustrated, that's what it was. She wanted Connor out of her kitchen. Out of her house. Preferably out of her life.

Connor had his hand under the foot. 'Try and push my hand away.' He rested his hand gently on the top. 'Pull up against my hand.' Then he began carefully but thoroughly to palpate all the tiny bones Kate knew a foot contained.

'Don't think anything's broken,' he said finally. 'But the only way to know for sure is to get an X-ray. Maybe I should run Bella back to A&E.'

'No need,' Kate said crisply. 'I can take her. I don't think riding a bike with a potentially broken foot is the best idea, do you?'

She didn't mean to sound like some prim school teacher but it certainly came out that way. She saw the look that Connor and Bella exchanged. Her niece was smiling.

'Don't take any notice,' Bella told Connor. 'She's a sweetheart, really.'

'I'm sure,' Connor murmured, sounding anything but sure. He backed away.

'Let me know how it goes,' he said by way of farewell.

Kate flicked off the controls on her stove. Dinner could wait. Her appetite had deserted her in any case.

'Come on.' She helped Bella down from the bench. 'You can sit a bit closer to floor level while I go and make myself presentable. Then we'll go and see what the damage is.'

The rest of the damage maybe. Something felt very odd about her home right now. As though something indefinable had been broken. Connor was gone but she could still feel his presence in her house.

And she didn't like the feeling one little bit.

3

'Connor! What are you doing here?'

Good question.

Connor wasn't quite sure of the answer, mind you. He should be playing squash with Mike the anaesthetist. Having a beer after the game and chewing the fat with the lads. He should, at least, be having his dinner.

But here he was in the emergency department of St Pat's. In a cubicle where Bella was lounging on the bed and Kate was sitting beside her, ramrod straight against the back of the chair.

No. This was Dr Graham sitting here. Connor sighed inwardly, knowing that this was largely why he had found himself drawn in this direction.

It was nearly an hour and a half since he'd left Bella sitting on the kitchen bench and he'd been out on the motorway, with the night air rushing past, while he'd tried to sort out the puzzle in his head.

The puzzle that Kate Graham represented.

The split personality.

Dr Graham. Prim and buttoned up at work. Closed off.

The house fitted with that image of her. Tasteful and perfect and so damned tidy. Like she was now, with her hair scraped back again and her glasses back in place and wearing a skirt and jacket that looked like the female equivalent of a business suit.

But he'd seen Kate and she'd been in frayed jeans and... and bare feet, for God's sake. And she'd had cute toes. With red nails.

Connor loved red toenails. He couldn't look at this woman now without remembering those toenails. He knew he wouldn't be able to pass her in the corridor of St Pat's from now on without remembering them, and it was messing with his head.

Two women in one body.

Connor was intrigued.

Not that he was attracted to her or anything. *Hell*, no. It was simply a conundrum.

A challenge.

He'd only come back to St Pat's because it was too late to jack up a game of squash and, if he was going to eat a microwaved dinner by himself, he wanted the distraction of the new journal he'd left on his desk. So why had he veered into the emergency department on his way out?

'I just wanted to hear the verdict on the foot,' he said aloud. 'If something's broken, I'll have a mountain of paperwork on the way. The theatre was booked under my name, you know.'

The foot was propped up on pillows, with an ice pack on the top of it.

'Look at this.' Bella leaned forward and lifted the ice pack.

The bruise was starting to look really impressive now. The colour was much darker and the internal bleeding was tracking down the side of the foot to pool in the hollow beneath the ankle bone.

'Hmm…' Connor said in his most professional voice.

Bella giggled.

Kate's voice was clipped. Clearly this was nothing to joke about. 'We've only just got back from X-Ray,' she said. 'We're waiting for the radiologist's report to come through.'

'I could pull up the X-ray and have a look myself if you like.' Connor was surprised they hadn't been fast-tracked in the first place.

Staff were always given preferential treatment and that was fine by him. It was one of the only perks of a job that required far more commitment than any other career.

'Bella's a patient here,' Kate said. 'And I'm a relative. The department's busy.'

She wasn't about to bend any rules herself and didn't want them bent for her.

Fine.

Connor smiled. He hitched one hip onto the end of Bella's bed.

'No worries,' he said. 'I've got nothing better to do. I'll wait, too.'

The discomfort on Kate's face was worth waiting a bit longer for some food. Man, she was regretting not bending a rule or two now. Her voice sounded tight when she spoke.

'I might go and give Jackie a call. She'll want an update.'

Connor raised an eyebrow when Kate pulled a mobile phone from the pocket of her jacket. She gave him the kind of look only women seemed to be capable of. The one that made you feel about two inches shorter or something.

'I'll go outside,' she told Bella. 'I wouldn't want to interfere with any electronic equipment being used in here.'

Connor grinned at Bella as Kate swept past. 'She does know that doctors have their phones on all the time in here as back-up for their pagers, doesn't she?'

Bella's eyes widened. 'Do they?'

'Of course they do.' Connor suppressed a sigh. Maybe it was just him. Maybe every other person on the St Pat's planet went around obeying every little rule and regulation. 'How's your foot feeling?'

'Fine. I had some painkillers when I got here. It doesn't even hurt to wiggle my toes now, see?'

Toes wiggled. Bella had a French polish thing going on. Classy. The sort of look he would have expected Kate to go for. If he'd ever bothered to spare a thought for her toenails.

Which he hadn't. Of course.

'Who's Jackie?' he asked abruptly.

'My mum. Kind of Kate's mum, too.'

'Oh?' Connor was bemused. Surely her niece's mother would be more in the category of a sister? 'How's that?'

'Kate came to live with us when she was fifteen. My dad's her older brother. I was six so it was like getting a big sister for a surprise present. A huge surprise, cos I didn't even know I had an aunt.'

'How come?'

Bella lowered her voice. 'Dad didn't have anything to do with his family. He left home when he was seventeen.'

'How old would Kate have been then?'

'About five? He's never talked about it. He doesn't talk about his family at all, really. Neither does Kate. It's like they're orphans or they've got a secret pact or something. Anyway, it was kind of cool to have a teenage aunt. Especially as I've got four younger brothers and sisters and if Kate hadn't come to live with us I would have been the oldest and had to help look after them all and that would have been a bit of a fun-buster, wouldn't it?'

Connor knew he shouldn't be encouraging this kind of personal gossip about a colleague but it was irresistible. There was clearly a mystery here. One that might explain why Kate was the way she was. Why had she gone to live with her older brother and his young family at an age when most girls needed their mothers? Why had her brother turned his back on his family when he hadn't been much older himself? What kind of parents had these young people had?

Connor wasn't going to try and analyse why he was so fascinated. He'd probably do that later, when he wasn't in the company of the irrepressible – and very open – Bella.

'So you've never met your grandparents?' he found himself asking quietly.

Bella shook her head. She bit her bottom lip as she sucked in a quick breath. 'Grandma died not that long after Kate came to live with us. She and Dad went off to her funeral and that was that. Except...'

'Except what?' Okay, Connor was dead curious now. Riveted, even.

'I shouldn't say... Kate doesn't even know I know.'

Connor leaned closer. 'I won't breathe a word,' he promised.

Bella was still hesitating. She looked over his shoulder as though fearful of Kate's return. Then she looked back at Connor, biting her lip. She wanted to tell him.

And, damn, he wanted to hear.

'You can trust me,' he murmured. 'So can Kate.'

'I found a letter,' Bella whispered. 'About a parole hearing.'

Connor's jaw dropped. 'Who was in prison?'

'I think he still is,' Bella said.

'Who?'

'My grandfather.'

'What's he in prison for?'

'I have no idea.' Bella shook her head. 'But I think he went in there the same year that Grandma died and that's... God, about seventeen years ago so it must have been something really bad—'

'What's really bad?'

They both jumped as Kate walked in.

'My foot,' Bella said promptly. 'If it's broken it would be a really bad way to be starting a new job.'

Connor had to admire the way Bella had extricated herself from a tricky moment, but something in Kate's face made him think that she knew there had been more to the conversation. The glance she flicked at Connor was wary. She would not be at all happy if she knew the kind of private details Bella had been sharing about her aunt, that was for sure. He shouldn't have encouraged it. He shouldn't even be here, come to that.

'I've just spoken to the consultant,' Kate said. 'He's had a good look at the X-ray and talked to the radiologist. Nothing's broken. He's going to come and talk to you before we go but they're going to put a compression bandage on and give you a sick note for work for a couple of days. You'll need to keep it elevated and rested. You might get a set of crutches if it's too painful to put weight on.'

'Not broken? Yay!' Bella beamed. 'I'll be dancing again in no time, then.'

A nurse bustled into the cubicle with a handful of bandages. 'Hi, I'm Gemma,' she said. 'I've come to bandage up that poor foot of yours.' She nodded at Kate and then did a double-take as she spotted the extra person in the cubicle. 'Connor! What are you doing here?'

'I'm kind of... involved in the case,' he said.

'Of course you are.' She grinned and turned to her patient. 'It's Bella, isn't it?'

'Yes.'

'And I hear you dropped a steriliser bucket on your foot in Theatre.'

'Mmm.'

'In my theatre,' Connor put in. For some reason he felt he needed to explain his involvement. He'd never dated Gemma but he had been out with one of her friends a few times. That knowing little comment was sending a message to Kate that he didn't like at all. He wasn't trying to pick Bella up, here. Not at all. She was bright and bubbly and fun and everything but she was far too young. And too... open? Not mysterious enough?

Uh-oh, there was something disturbing in this line of thought. It really was time he left but Gemma was uncovering Bella's foot now. He could just stay for a minute and make sure she did a good job of that compression bandage.

'Ooh, nice bruise,' Gemma said admiringly. 'Did I hear you say something about dancing soon?'

Bella was admiring her foot as well. 'Maybe not immediately.'

'Shame. There's a dance on next Saturday night that should be great fun.' Gemma looked up at Connor. 'I assume you'll be going.'

'Wasn't planning on it.'

This was another message he wasn't comfortable with Kate receiving. He could just imagine what she thought of him. Someone who took no notice of rules, dated everything in a skirt and couldn't stay away from even the hint of a party. Shallow only began to describe that kind of person, didn't it?

'But it's a fundraiser for Paeds. The "P" for Pool party?' Gemma shook her head, turning to Kate. 'The physiotherapy department is trying to raise enough money to put in a new therapeutic pool. You'll be going, won't you, Dr Graham?'

'No.'

The word was final. Kate had no intention of going to this party. Or any other party judging by the echo of the word that hung over Bella's bed.

A determined gleam came into Bella's eyes. 'Why not?' she demanded. 'Sounds fun. Except that I have no idea what a "P" party actually is. Sounds a bit dodgy to me.'

'Fancy dress,' Gemma explained. 'You have to come as a character that starts with the letter "P". You know, like a pirate?' She eyed Connor. 'That would be a great one for you.'

* * *

Kate was staring at her shoes. She didn't dare look at Connor.

She could understand all too well why the girls found him so attractive with that 'bad boy' vibe going on. It was all too easy to imagine him dressed up as a pirate with a gold ring in his ear and a rakish hat and a king-of-the-world kind of attitude.

No wonder she found Bella's face lighting up like a Christmas tree when she felt compelled to lift her gaze.

'What about a princess?' Bella exclaimed. 'Oh, I have to go. Even if I'm on crutches. I've always wanted an excuse to dress up as a princess.' She saw Kate's expression and grinned. 'Yeah, yeah... I know. I did it all the time when I was a kid but this would be like... legitimate.'

Kate had to smile at her excitement. She would make a perfect princess with her gorgeous long hair and those big blue eyes. The men would be falling all over themselves wanting to find out who she was. Maybe Connor should go as a prince instead of a pirate and stake a visible claim. She couldn't help her glance sliding in his direction as her brain prompted her to say something aloud, but the suggestion died on her lips at his expression.

Curious, that's what it was.

Oh, God... she just *knew* they'd been talking about her when she'd gone to phone Jackie. That conversation she'd interrupted hadn't been about Bella's shaky start to her new job at all. So what had been the 'really bad' thing they'd been discussing? How embarrassing it was to have a spinster aunt who hid herself away and needed to get a life?

'We've still got plenty of tickets,' Gemma said. She was winding a bandage firmly around Bella's foot with admirable precision. A figure-of-eight style, with the overlapping bandage edges exactly a centimetre from the previous one. 'There's an inter-departmental competition for who can sell the most tickets. You should all come.'

She turned her head to glare at Connor. 'Especially you. How could you not go when you're so involved with everything in the kids' wards?'

Connor was still staring at Kate. 'I'll go if Kate goes,' he said.

Bella laughed aloud. 'Yes! Me, too.'

Kate saw the look that passed between them. This was turning into a conspiracy. Not only had Bella hooked up with the hottest guy in St Pat's in no time flat, but had they also used the few minutes they'd had alone together to make some kind of pact to see that Bella's aunt... got a life?

'I'm not going,' Kate said, aware that she was failing to keep a hint of desperation from her tone. 'Fancy dress? I don't think so.'

'But don't you see?' Bella asked. 'It's perfect.'

'No, I don't see,' Kate muttered. She watched Gemma hook

the tiny metal 'crocodile' clips into place to secure Bella's bandage. Good. They could escape very soon.

'You never go to work social events, do you.' Bella was making a statement, not asking a question.

And it was true. Kate never did go to any social events. Not unless she absolutely had to. How embarrassing was this? Bella thought the whole world was on her side and there was no need to keep things private. She was open and honest and... everything Kate could never be.

No wonder Bella never had any trouble making friends wherever she went. Kate had nobody she could call a real friend but she didn't need that pointed out to the people she had to work with. Especially to Connor Matthews. It was bad enough that he already thought of her as boring and unattractive and incapable of having fun.

Bella didn't wait for a response. 'With a costume party you get to go as someone else. In a disguise. It doesn't really have to be you going at all.' She grinned at Connor. 'Hey, you could go as a priest.'

Gemma snorted. Even Kate felt her lips twitch.

Connor had spotted her amusement. 'Pollyanna starts with "P",' he muttered.

'You wouldn't need to dress up,' Gemma said kindly. 'Pathologist starts with "P". You could wear your white coat maybe.'

The one that she wore all buttoned up, like she buttoned up her life? Prim was a 'P' word. So was prude. Kate felt the stirrings of real annoyance. She felt she was being put under pressure to prove she wasn't that person. Which she could, if she wanted to. With bells on. Prostitute started with 'P'. She could borrow that scrap of fabric Bella called a skirt and put some bright red lipstick on and leave her hair loose and nobody would recognise her.

Good grief... the prospect was disturbingly attractive.

Except that Connor would recognise her because he'd seen her with her hair down. He might think she was trying to send the message that she was up for it. Desperate, even.

It was a relief when the ED consultant breezed in to talk to Bella and broke the negative spin her thoughts were taking. He had a pair of elbow crutches with him and advised Bella to use them for the next day or so until she could bear weight without pain.

And then it was finally time to go home and get to their long-delayed dinner. Thankfully, Connor was preparing to disappear into the night, after saying he was glad things had turned out okay so that he wouldn't have to cope with long-winded serious accident investigations.

But he waited to hold the door open for Bella, who was hopping slowly as she got used to the crutches, and Gemma came rushing up with a bunch of tickets in her hand.

'So... three tickets for you guys, then?' she asked brightly.

Connor eyed Kate. 'I will if you will,' he said.

'I can't go if neither of you go,' Bella said. 'I don't know anybody else here well enough yet.' She also eyed Kate. 'Please? Please, please, please, Auntie Katie?'

Auntie Katie? Kate stifled a groan. That took her back to the days when her niece had been a small child and Kate had had something that Bella had wanted very badly.

Kate shook her head, realising that defeat was looming. 'We'll see.'

'That always means yes.'

'No,' Kate said faintly. 'It doesn't. But we'll buy the tickets anyway seeing it's for such a good cause.'

Bella somehow got a hand free to give Connor a high five. 'We'll see you there.'

* * *

She was here.

Connor hadn't really expected Kate to turn up but his reaction should have been no more than surprise, surely? Why was he feeling so pleased?

Just to be on the safe side, he avoided her for the first hour or two of the party but even when he was in the middle of the dance floor, he couldn't help spotting her at regular intervals. What on earth was she wearing? A long black dress that had wide strips of white material pinned across it at regular intervals. Was she supposed to be... a prisoner?

That would be a bit Freudian, wouldn't it?

And didn't convicts have arrows rather than stripes?

He could ask Bella but she was floating around in a pretty, puffy pink dress and a sparkly tiara and was never short of a dance or conversational partner. Kate always seemed to have someone to talk to as well. Who was that guy in the panda suit?

Oh, yes... Lewis Blackman, head of the pathology department. Not that it was any of his business but Connor noted that they seemed to be getting on very well and he found himself frowning. For goodness' sake, Lewis was far too old for Kate. He was at least sixty and Kate couldn't be any more than around his own age.

He didn't see Kate dancing. Not even once.

Bella must have noticed her aunt's lack of participation as well because when Connor finally had the opportunity to dance with the best-looking princess of the night, she turned him down.

'Ask Kate,' she urged.

Connor was about to say 'No way' but something in Bella's gaze stopped the words emerging.

'Please?' Bella added. She twinkled at him, rather like the imitation diamonds in her tiara.

'Fine,' Connor growled reluctantly. 'I'll dance with the prisoner.'

'Prisoner?'

'That's what her costume is, isn't it?'

Bella laughed. 'No! She's being a pedestrian crossing.'

Connor was still grinning as he made his way to where Kate was still talking to Lewis. A pedestrian crossing. Smart. Different.

He liked that.

He extended a hand as he got closer. 'May I have the pleasure...?'

Kate shook her head. 'Thanks, but I don't dance.'

No surprises there.

What was surprising was that Lewis Blackman made a growling sound that Connor could have easily produced himself.

'Go on, Kate,' Lewis urged. 'Let your hair down for once.'

Connor wished she had done that in a far more literal sense. He'd seen that astonishing fall of silky black hair but it was all buttoned up again right now. Not in the usual braid she wore at work but kind of folded into a complicated knot thing at the back of her head. Something looked different about her, though... Her face looked softer.

Make-up?

No. She had ditched her glasses again, that's what it was. He could see her eyes clearly. He saw the way they widened at Lewis's rather abrupt instruction. He saw a cloud of, what... hurt? Embarrassment?

A hint of fear, even?

He could deal with that. He caught Kate's hand and smiled.

'How 'bout if I say please? Or perhaps please, please, please?'

* * *

How could anybody refuse an offer like that?

Kate could feel so many people watching her. She could sense the astonishment mixed with envy that was coming from all the women nearby. Connor had gone the whole hog with a pirate costume. The wild wig with its braids and beads and a red bandanna. A flowing white shirt with its cuffs carelessly unbuttoned. More flowing white fabric as a sash that had a knife in a scabbard attached to it. Knee-high black boots. A heavy layer of eyeliner and the dusting of authentic designer stubble completed the look to perfection.

He looked every inch a pirate. Dark and dangerous and... quite simply devastatingly attractive.

And here he was, holding the hand of the person with the least imaginative costume here. All Kate had done had been to tack some strips of an old white sheet to the only formal dress she possessed, which was, of course, a classic black number.

Any woman in her right mind would jump at the chance to dance with Connor. They had been all evening. Kate knew that because, despite her very best intentions, she had found her gaze drawn to him time after time and he'd been with a different partner on every occasion. She had told herself she had just been waiting to see him dance with Bella but when he'd finally approached her niece, Bella had clearly refused. Bella was now being led onto the dance floor by someone dressed as Pinocchio, but she caught Kate's glance and waved. No. It was more like a signal that it was high time Kate joined in the fun.

Even Lewis was staring at her with a vaguely perplexed expression. He'd sounded almost exasperated in ordering her to go and dance and 'let her hair down for once'.

For once? Did her boss think she needed to get a life as well?

Kate could have dealt with whatever negative impressions everyone around her had if she'd stuck to her guns and refused to make an idiot of herself on the dance floor. She had every intention of doing exactly that until the moment when Connor took her hand.

That smile.

It went with the expression in his eyes that said very clearly, *I understand... you can trust me.*

Feeling somewhat stunned, Kate allowed herself to be led onto the dance floor.

For probably the first time in her life, accepting the invitation of a man and thereby relinquishing control didn't feel like a personal threat.

It felt curiously like a gift.

* * *

Holding Kate in his arms on the dance floor felt exactly the way Connor would have expected it to feel.

It would have been much easier if the music had been a bit faster. He could have kept more of a distance between their bodies and given Kate a twirl or two and it might have been fun to shake her up a little. But here he was, dancing to quite a slow track with a woman he didn't understand and didn't even like.

Dr Graham was following his lead but she was trying to keep her steps and her posture perfect and avoid eye contact. It felt stilted and awkward.

There was only one way he could get through this, Connor decided. He closed his eyes, tugged Kate more firmly into his arms and let the music take over.

* * *

This was so hard it was unbearable.

Kate knew how to dance. Once upon a time, so far back in her life it was totally irrelevant now, she had loved letting go and allowing music to flow through her body. To drift with its current.

But it was impossible now. She couldn't even hear the music because her senses were overloaded with the effort it was taking to distance herself from how it felt to be held in a man's arms.

She could do this. She *had* done it, time and again. There was a place in her head she could go where she became kind of an observer of what was happening to her body. Good grief, she was capable of having sex with a man from the perspective of that place and she was quite confident her partner had not been aware of her emotional isolation.

So why couldn't she get into it right now?

Her senses were overloaded. The warmth of Connor's body. The way her clothing was offering no kind of protection and making it feel as if his hands were burning imprints into bare skin. The musky male smell of him. The easy, confident flow to the way he moved.

When Connor pulled her even closer, Kate shut her eyes and tried harder but, oddly, what happened was that she could hear the music now. Something about the way he was moving to it maybe. He had more than simply natural rhythm. There was a sensitivity to the way he moved that made it feel like he was channelling the music.

Something melted inside Kate that she hadn't even known was frozen. Instead of the hold of those arms feeling like prison bars, it became a kind of force field. Something safe that begged her to relax into it. A combination of beautiful music and human touch that was pure pleasure.

And it was irresistible.

* * *

Connor felt the moment that Kate relaxed in his arms.

She could really *dance*. He went from feeling he was hauling a concrete block around the dance floor to having something weightless in his arms. He could lose himself in the music and have every move followed as though he was dancing with his own shadow, and it was... amazing.

The track didn't last nearly long enough. Connor didn't want another dance partner tonight. He wanted to dance with Kate again. And again. He'd never felt that kind of connection with a woman before, on or off a dance floor.

Wow... If she was like this to dance with, he couldn't begin to imagine what she might be like in bed.

But whatever the astonishing connection had been, it ended when the music faded, and the ending was harsh. As abrupt as a light switch being flicked off.

For a split second, Kate had stayed as close to his body as it was possible to be in public, as though she hadn't realised that the track had finished. But then she jerked back. She met his gaze for only a heartbeat but it was long enough for Connor to see the way she refocused and actually saw *him*.

The way her eyes darkened with unmistakeable fear.

Terror, even?

'I... have to go.' The words came out in a whisper.

And then she turned and all but fled from his side. She disappeared amongst the crowd of people and Connor was far too slow in trying to follow.

By the time he made it off the dance floor and went looking for her, Kate had apparently left the building.

4

This was *not* his problem.

Okay. Someone had obviously done a number on Kate Graham and made her afraid of men.

But it wasn't *him*, dammit, so it had been totally undeserved to have her look at him like that. As if he was some kind of monster, for God's sake, like a murderer or rapist.

Well, he wasn't going to let it happen again. It had been easy enough to avoid her at work in the last few days since that fundraising fancy-dress ball. She didn't have to work most weekends and he'd kept strictly to his expected areas of the hospital since then. His path had crossed with Bella's up in the theatre suite but that hadn't been a problem. He'd simply avoided talking to Kate's niece as well. Apart from that he'd attended an outpatient clinic or two and spent the rest of his time in the wards.

He was heading for one of those wards right now to see thirteen-year-old Estelle Montgomery, who'd been admitted after breaking her leg very early that morning.

Tall for her age, Estelle had the tanned skin and bleached

blonde hair of someone who spent more time on a beach than anywhere else. Her mother was also in the room and they were both flicking through a magazine. The pages seemed to be a feature on bikinis.

Nice. Connor stopped himself from making any appreciative sounds, however. Instead he smiled.

'Hi. I'm Connor Matthews.'

'Oh…' The magazine slid from her hands and Estelle's mother swallowed visibly. 'You're the orthopaedic surgeon Stella's been admitted under.'

Connor nodded. 'I'm sorry I haven't had a chance to say hello before this but I hope my registrar and the rest of the staff have been looking after you well?'

It was Estelle who nodded. 'Everyone's been cool. I asked if I could get a proper cast on and go home but they said I had to wait for you to come and see me.'

She glanced towards the window of her room. 'It's a great day. I know it'll be a few weeks before I can get wet but if I got out now and didn't have to go to school, I could at least go and watch the others.'

Her chin wobbled slightly as she looked at her mother. 'Couldn't I? You wouldn't mind an hour or two on the beach, would you, Mum? Shane's practising for the competition next weekend and…'

Her mother's smile was strained. 'Let's see what Dr Matthews has to say first, Stella.'

Connor was looking at the long, tanned leg, which had been left free of the bed cover. Cradled in a plaster shell, the malformation of the fracture was clearly visible halfway down the shin.

'How's the pain?'

Estelle shrugged. 'It's fine if I don't move.'

Her mother sighed. 'She doesn't admit to anything that might stop her getting near the sea. She dislocated her elbow a couple of years ago and still went back to catch another wave.'

Connor smiled at Estelle. 'Surfing, huh?'

Estelle's face lit up. 'I won the thirteen and under section that year. That's why I was up so early today. The waves are always good at dawn and I'm practising for this year's competition.'

'Wow.' Connor shook his head. 'The longest I've managed to stay upright on a surfboard was about ten seconds.'

'It just takes practice. And good balance. Learning to dance helps. I started when I was about three and I still do classes whenever I can. Can you dance?'

'Stella!' Her mother sounded shocked. 'You can't ask Dr Matthews that sort of thing.'

Connor grinned. 'Of course she can. And, yes, I like dancing.'

He'd always liked dancing but it hit him suddenly that he might not like it as much from now on. The way he'd felt dancing with Kate had been like nothing he'd ever experienced before, and he had this curious certainty that he never would again.

The way she'd felt in his arms.

That connection.

The sheer power of something sensual that was so big Connor couldn't recognise it. So alluring he hadn't been able to stop thinking about it since. He'd tried to tell himself he'd imagined it, but what if he hadn't?

What if there was something he hadn't known was missing from his life because he hadn't even known it existed?

And what if it only existed because the other half of the equation had been Kate?

Connor actually shook his head again to clear the fleeting distraction. Estelle's mother noticed the subtle movement and drew in an audible breath.

'There's something wrong, isn't there? That's why Stella couldn't just get plaster on her leg and go home?'

Connor had been planning on introducing himself, examining Estelle and then taking her mother somewhere for a private conversation. Both mother and daughter were staring at him now and then they looked at each other.

'I don't want you talking behind my back,' Estelle said firmly. 'It's my leg and I want to know what's wrong with it.'

Her mother caught Connor's gaze. 'Stella's thirteen, going on thirty,' she said with a wry smile. 'There's no point hiding anything. And it's just the two of us. Stella's dad died when she was a baby.'

With a slow nod Connor took an X-ray from the folder he was carrying. He held it up so that the light from the window shone through it.

'You know you've broken your tibia, which is the bigger of the two bones in your lower leg. The fracture itself isn't that serious, although it's bad enough to need a pin to stabilise it. What worried the doctors in the emergency department initially was that it hadn't been caused by any trauma. You were just climbing some steps, yes?'

Estelle nodded. 'I heard it snap. It was really gross.'

'You hadn't had a knock from your surfboard or anything before that?'

'No.'

'It's not brittle bones or something, is it?' her mother asked. 'It can't be, surely. She gets knocked all the time. That surfboard is bigger than she is and she goes out in some wild waves sometimes.'

'For a bone to break without trauma being involved means there's something wrong,' Connor agreed. 'And when this X-ray was taken it showed a mass in the tibia. Can you see the way the line of the bone isn't straight on the edge there? And how much wider the whole bone is in that spot than above and below it?'

'A... mass?' The word from Estelle's mother was a horrified whisper.

'What's a mass?' Estelle queried. She was staring at her mother. 'Oh, my God... you mean, like... *cancer*?'

Connor's heart sank at the fear in their voices, but he couldn't be any less than honest. 'A mass is when cells are growing and dividing in a manner that isn't normal. A collection of abnormal cells like this is called a tumour. We don't know yet whether the tumour is benign or cancerous. Given your history, Estelle, and what we know of your general state of health so far, the chances are very good that this tumour is benign.'

'You'll do a biopsy, right?' Estelle was nodding. 'I've seen it on telly.'

'We'll certainly do a biopsy and find out exactly what we're dealing with. Because you already need surgery to pin the fracture, that's when we'll do the biopsy. I'm going to send you for an MRI first, though.'

'Why?'

'It's an advanced test that can show better detail of not only the bone but all the soft tissue around it, including tendons and nerves and muscles and things. It can show us whether this tumour is confined to the bone.'

Connor paused for a moment, letting the implications sink in. 'Normally, we'd do a biopsy and if we didn't like the kind of cells we found we'd look at a course of chemotherapy or radiotherapy to shrink the tumour before surgery. Depending on what we find, the better course of action may be to remove the tumour during surgery and use chemo later if it's necessary.'

'How much of the bone do you have to remove?' Estelle's mother asked quietly.

'That will depend on what we find. If it's benign, only enough to allow your leg to continue growing as normally as possible. If it's cancerous, it will depend on both the type of cancer and whether it's spread.'

Connor didn't want to go into details about the more aggressive types of bone cancer unless he had to when the diagnosis was confirmed. He gave Estelle's mother a steady glance. 'I know it's a big ask but right now the consent form you need to sign allows me to take what I consider the best course of action depending on what we find during surgery.'

Estelle was gripping a fold of her sheet in her hands. 'I thought I was just going to have to stop surfing for a few weeks and that I'd have crutches and a cast that the kids at school could write stuff on. That was bad enough but I could deal with it.'

The fold of sheet twisted in her hands and she gave a huge sniff. 'I'm scared, Mum...' she sobbed. 'I'd rather die than have my leg cut off.'

'Don't say that.' The older woman was close to tears herself now as she reached to hold her daughter in her arms.

Connor couldn't deny that amputation was a possibility and it was something they needed to talk about. He had a dozen things to get sorted before slotting this emergency case into his surgery schedule for the day but there was no way he could leave until he had provided enough reassurance to reduce some of his patient's fear.

The possibility was extremely remote that Estelle would have to lose her leg but if that was what it would take to save her life, that was what Connor would have to do. He perched a hip on the end of the bed and settled in to talk for as long as it was going to take. At least it was still early in the day. Some people wouldn't have even started work yet. People who had cushy jobs, maybe.

Like pathologists?

A nurse poked her head around the door but Connor sent her away with a glance. He could keep an eye on whatever needed monitoring, like the circulation in Estelle's foot. Reaching out, he touched the skin. It was a bit cool but his fingers found a strong pulse on the top of her foot and he kept them there for a few moments to check her heart rate.

* * *

He was touching her.

His hand was on the bare skin of her neck. It tracked the bumps of her spine, ran beneath the angle of her shoulder blade, and then the trickle of exquisite sensation moved relentlessly on to touch the curve of her breast. His fingers spread to cup the soft swell of flesh, and the ball of his thumb grazed her nipple.

The shaft of pleasure was so intense it was painful.

The pain of heightened desire was enough to wake Kate. The sheets were tangled around her and she was gasping for air.

She rolled out of bed and headed for the shower, but the dream lingered in the shape of the deep burning that was a desire she had never experienced in a conscious state. She didn't want to experience it, awake or asleep. It was pure sensation. Uncontrollable.

Destructive.

Oh... God. Even turning the shower control to sluice her body with icy-cold water wasn't enough to douse the effects of that dream.

She shouldn't have danced with Connor.

Somehow, something had been unleashed that night. Kate had recognised it at the moment it had happened and she'd gone into damage control mode by tearing herself away and then putting as much distance as possible between herself and the man who had turned the key to unlock that forbidden space.

She had caught whatever it was and thought she'd locked it safely away, but her subconscious was betraying her.

Every night.

Kate got dressed in a tailored blouse and pencil-thin skirt. She brushed her hair and scraped it back into a tight ponytail before braiding the length until there was just enough hair to keep the rubber band in place. She even looped the braid and used another hair tie to hold the loops securely. She didn't want a braid swinging free on her back today. She didn't want anything swinging free, including unwanted feelings, and at least she knew she was in control now that she was awake.

A quick breakfast and then Kate intended heading in to work. She had a teaching session scheduled in the lab and hopefully, on either side of that, a day that would be busy enough to keep her fully occupied, physically and mentally.

Bella stumbled sleepily into the kitchen, wearing a singlet top and boxer shorts as Kate was mashing an avocado onto half a toasted bagel.

'Ooh... yum. Not. Any coffee?'

'Help yourself. I'm having a raspberry tea.'

'You're so healthy.'

It sounded like a complaint. Kate eyed her niece. 'Maybe

some of my healthy lifestyle will rub off on you. Looks like you could use it.'

'I'm fine. Day off. All I have to do is go in this afternoon to get my new roster. I just got up to keep you company.'

Bella smiled and the sun came out in the kitchen. Kate felt herself softening in the glow. How could anybody resist a smile like that? She watched Bella as she pushed a tumble of blonde hair over her shoulder and yawned hugely as she reached for a coffee mug. Even half dressed and half asleep with yesterday's mascara smudged around her eyes she was an extraordinarily beautiful young woman.

'Late night?'

'Did I wake you? Sorry.'

'No. You look like you could use a bit more sleep, that's all.'

'Hmm. Might go back to bed for a bit. I wasn't that late. I met some nurses from St Pat's at a pub near the hospital. We just had a couple of drinks, that's all.' She glanced at Kate. 'Connor was there.'

'Oh?' Kate suddenly had difficulty swallowing her mouthful. She concentrated on reaching for her cup of tea. What was Bella going to tell her next? That she and Connor were now officially dating? Oh... help. That would mean she would be seeing more of him. Bella might even bring him home for the night.

She couldn't deal with that. With the kind of dreams she had haunting her nights at the moment, the thought of Connor here, in bed with Bella, touching her... well, it was almost obscene. And as absurd as it was, there was the possibility that she could end up feeling jealous of her beloved niece. Bella was the person she loved most in the whole world. Kate couldn't let something like this threaten such a precious relationship.

She cleared her throat. 'You know, it might be timely to talk about a few house rules.'

'Oh?' Bella unconsciously echoed her aunt's neutral tone. 'You mean like putting the top back on the toothpaste and stuff?'

'I'm thinking more about visitors.'

Bella was stirring sugar into her coffee. 'I'm not following.'

'Dates,' Kate said succinctly. 'Men. In particular, men that might want to stay overnight.'

Bella grinned. 'I try and stick to one at a time but, hey, you go for it, Auntie Kate. More power to you.'

Kate's cup clanked loudly on the saucer as she put it down. 'I'm not talking about me, Bella. I'm talking about you. And Connor. I don't want to wake up and find him in my kitchen. If you want to stay the night with him, do it at his place, okay?'

Pushing herself to her feet, Kate tipped half a cup of tea down the sink and abandoned her half-eaten bagel on the bench. Bella was staring at her, open-mouthed.

'You're kidding, right?'

'No.' Kate plucked her jacket from where she'd hung it over the back of her chair and started to put it on.

Bella was shaking her head. 'You *must* be kidding.'

'Why's that?' Kate hated how snappy she sounded but it was a warning all on its own. This was dangerous territory. She had to take control.

Bella had a curious expression on her face. A half-smile that suggested a wisdom beyond both her years and her personality.

'Because it's not me Connor's interested in,' she said slowly. 'It's *you*.'

The wave of longing was unexpected. Debilitating, almost. Kate was having trouble getting her arm through the sleeve of her jacket. The knot filled her belly. Tight and painful and... pointless.

'Don't be ridiculous.' If her previous comment had been a

snap, this would verge on being a snarl, but Bella only snorted softly. The sound was one of amusement.

'I wasn't the only one who noticed the chemistry between you two when you were dancing the other night. It's as plain as this mountain of a zit I've got erupting on my chin.' Bella fingered the spot. 'Good grief... I'm not a teenager any more. It's not fair.'

'Stop thinking like a teenager, then,' was all Kate could manage to say. 'And seeing things that aren't – and never will be – there. And have some fruit for breakfast,' she threw over her shoulder as she headed for the briefcase waiting for her by the door. 'I'll see you later. I'm going to work.'

* * *

The labs were humming.

All the usual work was in full swing, with samples of all kinds being tested, reports dictated and results being dispatched. Lewis Blackman was using the time before he started the day's scheduled autopsies to rove the area and make sure that his department was running like clockwork.

Every microscope in the large room was in use, both by technicians on duty and the members of the tutorial group of junior doctors that Kate was instructing. She was following up her lecture by testing how much her students had taken in. Her boxes of teaching slides were spread over counters and eager young medics were trying to outdo each other by identifying what they could see.

'What have you got there, Neil?'

'I think it's an osteoid osteoma.'

'Which is?'

'A common, benign, bone-producing neoplasm. Predominantly found in males aged between ten and twenty years.'

'Common sites?'

'Fifty per cent are found in the femur or tibia.'

'What's the differential diagnosis?'

'An aggressive osteoblastoma, which is also benign. Or an osteosarcoma.'

'Why is it important to differentiate them?'

'An osteosarcoma is one of the most aggressive and highly lethal tumours and commonly throws metastases to the lungs and liver.'

'How can you be sure this isn't an osteosarcoma?'

'Because I can see the lesional tissue. The nidus. It's well demarcated from the surrounding bone.' The student moved to let Kate lean over the microscope.

She nodded and then looked up. 'Anyone got a slide that shows an osteosarcoma?'

'I have, I think.' It was a registrar called Marie who spoke. 'It looks like lace.'

Kate checked the second slide. 'Right. I want everyone to look at both these examples and then we'll have a quick recap on differential diagnoses and clinical behaviour for both types of tumours.'

'Kate?' A technician edged into the group. 'Janet's on the theatre run but due to get a piece of kidney from Theatre One. There's an urgent case in Theatre Three. Bone biopsy being done on a thirteen-year-old girl. The surgery hasn't started yet but do you want me to go and wait to collect the specimen?'

'Please. And bring it to me.' Kate eyed her group of students again. 'This is timely. You can see a real-time investigation on a bone biopsy. If it's happening during surgery, the results are critical. It might mean the difference between losing or saving a limb.'

The group was milling between the two microscopes and debating clinical information when an alarm sounded a few minutes later.

'Oh, no...' It didn't take much to trigger a fire alarm in a hospital and the disruption could be disastrous. Kate flicked a glance around her busy department. Could she afford to ignore it?

Someone rushed into the laboratory area. 'There's smoke coming from the kitchens,' he shouted. 'Everybody out.'

'Oh, my God...' Marie was looking terrified. 'We'll be caught in the basement. How do we get out?'

'Follow me.' Neil reached for her hand, his arm knocking the tray of slides on the bench beside her. It tipped, sending some of the precious samples Kate had collected over many years into a puddle of broken glass.

There were so many people moving now. Lewis was trying to marshal everybody to leave in an orderly fashion but some were desperately trying to finish or pause the tests they were running and others were moving equipment or samples to protect them in case the overhead sprinklers came on. Many of her students were stuffing notes into satchels and trying to find their other personal items. Lewis was looking in her direction. He looked pale, Kate noticed, and he was rubbing the top of his left arm as if it hurt.

'Leave everything,' Kate ordered. She could smell the smoke herself now. 'There's no time.' She waited by the door to make sure everyone got out of the department, including Lewis.

'Are you all right?' she asked her boss as he joined the people filing through the door.

'I'm fine. Let's get going. It's probably only some burnt toast or something but we can't take the risk.'

They were all hurrying now. Kate heard a crash and the tinkle of more broken glass as something else was knocked over. More of her collection of slides? She could also hear the faint wail of sirens coming from a distance.

With her heart sinking, Kate followed her colleagues to the evacuation point. Her day had just officially turned to custard.

* * *

Connor was taking his time, scrubbing in with meticulous attention to detail.

His hands were already red from the pressure of the soap-impregnated bristles and now he was concentrating on the points between his fingers. He could hear the familiar sounds of the operating theatre being set up – trolleys being wheeled into position, the clink of metal instruments being laid out.

Those sterile instruments would include a bone saw that Connor desperately hoped he wouldn't have to use to remove the lower part of Estelle's leg, but the MRI scan had been inconclusive. He'd been hoping to see a well-defined margin to the tumour that would indicate that it had been slow-growing enough for the bone to respond to its presence. If it had been there he could have been virtually certain that they were dealing with a benign growth and he could have gone into this surgery with justifiable optimism.

Instead, he had a gnawing anxiety that was uncharacteristic.

'Hey, Connor.' A nurse had his sterile towel ready for when he'd rinsed the soap from his hands and forearms. 'I saw you the other night. You make a great pirate.'

Connor merely grunted, angling his hands under the

stream of warm water. He didn't want to talk about the other night. He was having enough trouble trying to stop thinking about it as it was.

Part of it, anyway.

The way Kate had looked at him. He'd been shocked, that's what it was. One minute she was in his arms and he'd been encased in an extraordinary sensation of... of...

Connor sighed, reaching for the towel. No. He still couldn't define what that feeling had been. It had held a warmth that had been pure comfort but also a thrill that had been a precursor of ecstasy. Above all, there'd been a feeling of something being completely... right. As if the last piece of the world's most complicated jigsaw puzzle had been slotted into place. He couldn't summon up the sensation again so it had become even more elusive. Unattainable.

And ultimately desirable.

Not that there was any point in even thinking about it. It might have been there, but when Kate had pulled away and given him that look of horror, it had been doused as effectively as if someone had dumped a bucket of icy water on his head.

Had she felt it too?

But why would you run away from it?

Connor simply didn't understand. Just like he couldn't understand the random bad luck that a thirteen-year-old girl who lived to surf and dance might have to lose a part of her body that made it possible to live her dreams. The knot in his gut tightened a notch or two. He could only hope for the best. And do his best for Estelle. The technician from the pathology lab was already standing by, looking nervous in the corner of the theatre. Well, she'd have to wait for a while to collect the specimen. If Connor had been meticulous about scrubbing in, it was nothing compared to how he was about to tackle this potentially life-altering surgery.

He'd be sending a message that the most senior pathologist available needed to examine the specimen, too. He would remove as much of the tumour as he could but the pathologist would have to X-ray and then thinly section the specimen to identify the lesional tissue. It would be Connor's turn to stand by then, in case the pathologist needed a bigger sample. If there was any chance of a diagnosis that this was a benign osteoid osteoma, Connor was more than prepared to wait as long as it took. It was a damn shame they were still dithering about finding the funding to have a permanent pathology area up and running right here in the theatre suite so that samples could be processed faster.

Mind you, if they did, they would have a pathologist in the department for every case like this and he might find himself working a lot more closely with Kate.

Would he want to see her almost every day?

No.

Yes.

Maybe.

Some time later, Connor decided he would be prepared to deal with having Kate close by for the convenience factor. Waiting for the result took far too long. Apparently there'd been a fire alarm in the basement area of St Pat's because some idiotic kitchen hand had left a stack of tea towels on top of a glowing element on a stove. Even after taking his time to remove the specimen, it had been a forty-five-minute wait to get the result phoned through.

And it didn't take nearly long enough because when that result came through, it was the worst possible outcome. Estelle had an aggressive osteosarcoma and it extended beyond the margins of the bone already removed.

With a heart much heavier than the bone saw he requested from his scrub nurse, Connor moved on to the next phase of what was now a heartbreaking operation.

* * *

Kate surveyed the chaos that was still reigning in her laboratory.

Not only was there equipment out of place, but they were still cleaning up broken glass and someone was mopping up blood. Coming back for her possessions, Marie had slipped on something wet and had fallen, cutting her hand quite badly on a shattered test tube.

Technicians were coming up to her constantly asking what to do about tests that had been interrupted and whether new samples would have to be obtained. The X-ray equipment had been malfunctioning when an urgent biopsy sample had come down from Theatre and it took a while to discover that a fuse had been tripped during the alarm with power being cut off to various points. Kate had sectioned the sample herself and dismissed the students in favour of doing the diagnosis with her own registrar, Mark, because it was no longer a good time to include the young doctors in the process. There was simply too much other troubleshooting that needed to be done.

It was at that point that Kate noticed Lewis again. The head of department should have been in the same kind of firefighting mode she was in herself, restoring calm to the chaos in here, but he was standing to one side of the large area, looking preoccupied. And... grey. He wasn't rubbing his arm any longer. Instead, he had a hand pressed to the centre of his chest.

Kate was by his side in seconds. 'You've got chest pain, haven't you?'

Lewis nodded.

'Radiation?'

'Left arm. And jaw.' It sounded as if it was hard for Lewis to say anything. As if he was in excruciating pain. He was sweating, too. He had all the classic symptoms of someone who was suffering a heart attack.

'Run,' she ordered a young technician. 'Find the nearest wheelchair or trolley. I've got to get Dr Blackman up to the emergency department. Try Medical Records.'

Wheelchairs were often abandoned outside the medical-record department after someone had delivered a heavy load of notes. If she could transport Lewis herself, Kate knew it would be a lot faster than waiting for an orderly. And time mattered if Lewis was having a heart attack. With every passing minute more of his heart muscle could be being destroyed.

Her registrar was clearing an area near one of the microscopes she had been using with her students, clearly preparing to finish the bone biopsy examination. Mark was fairly new to the department and the specialty but he was competent enough. Nonetheless, Kate should sign the diagnosis off herself but...

But Lewis could be dying here. He was her boss. Her mentor. A dear friend.

And the technician had just rushed back into the lab with a wheelchair.

'I'll be back as soon as possible,' Kate told Mark. 'Carry on. If there's any doubt at all about the diagnosis, wait for me.'

* * *

It didn't take very long to deliver Lewis to the emergency department.

He was rushed straight into a resus area. An oxygen mask and electrodes were on him within seconds. A registrar was gaining IV access to administer pain relief and a nurse produced GTN spray and an aspirin tablet for Lewis to chew and swallow.

'We're onto it,' the staff assured Kate as she stood watching.

'Go,' Lewis urged. 'You're needed downstairs.'

'I'll be back as soon as I can,' Kate promised. 'Hang in there.'

By the time she got back to the basement of St Pat's, the results for Theatre Three had just been phoned through.

'What was it?'

'Oesteosarcoma,' Mark told her grimly. 'Classic. Late stage.'

'*What*? But the X-ray...' Kate cleared her stunned reaction with a single, sharp shake of her head. 'Show me.'

Sure enough, the microscopic evidence was clearly that of an aggressive, malignant tumour.

That poor kid, Kate thought. Thirteen years old and she was probably going to lose her leg. Or would they wait and give her a course of chemo before operating again?

They?

It would be Connor holding the scalpel up there. He was a specialist in paediatric bone cancer. The best. At least the girl had the chance of having her life saved, if not her leg.

She still couldn't believe it. She pulled the slide free from its clips, wanting to see another one. To gather more evidence. It was then that she noticed something that made her blood run cold.

A tiny dot on the corner of the slide. A marker. The kind she always used on the slides she kept for her teaching.

Time seemed to stop and yet Kate's brain – and her hands –

were moving at the speed of light. It took only seconds to confirm the worst. Somehow, one of her teaching slides had become mixed up with the new sample from Theatre.

The thirteen-year-old girl didn't have a highly aggressive cancer at all. The tumour was benign and could be easily treated.

Kate ran to the phone and dialled the Theatre extension. The phone rang. And rang. What was keeping someone from answering? Were they all too busy? Doing an unnecessary amputation?

Kate shoved the phone at the nearest technician. 'Wait till someone answers,' she snapped. 'Tell them to stop. They've got the wrong diagnosis.'

She couldn't just wait. Kate ran for the door, unbuttoning her coat as she went so that she could move faster.

She was fit. Four flights of stairs would only take a minute. She would take them two at a time. Three, if she could.

This couldn't be happening.

Not on her watch.

* * *

Connor had delayed for longer than he should have. Looking at the MRI scans again. Trying to decide just how high up they needed to go to try and get past the potential spread of the lethal cancer. He called in a paediatric oncology consultant to discuss whether to deal with the fracture and wait for Estelle to undergo a course of chemotherapy before the irreversible step of amputation.

But the decision had been made.

Connor picked up the bone saw and tested it. The whine reminded him of a dentist's drill. Just before it hit an exposed nerve in a tooth. For a few seconds the sound had drowned out the faint ring of the telephone in the technician's booth that nobody seemed to be in a hurry to answer. Grimly, he put the saw down and picked up a scalpel. He needed to fully expose the bone he was going to be cutting through. Scalpel poised, Connor was astonished to see the double doors leading into the theatre burst open. Someone was standing there, holding a mask to her face with its unfastened strings dangling loose. She wore a white coat.

Unbuttoned, but it was obviously Kate. Her eyes were wide and frightened and she was panting so hard she could barely speak.

'*Stop...*' she managed. 'You have to stop.'

5

'You can't blame yourself.'

'Of course I can.' Kate couldn't stop pacing. She was in the living room of her house, a long room that had windows and a set of French doors that led to a small courtyard and lawn bordered by the big old trees that covered the property.

It was 7 p.m. but still full daylight. A lovely summery day that showed no sign of ending yet. It had, without doubt, been the longest day of Kate's life. She groaned aloud.

'It's my department. With Lewis out of action I have to take full responsibility for what happens in there.'

Bella was curled up on the sofa, watching her aunt with a concerned frown on her face. 'It wasn't your fault there was a fire alarm and things got messed up.'

'I should have been doing the biopsy. Mark doesn't have enough experience. He couldn't see that there was an anomaly. He didn't go back and double-check.'

'You weren't there to do the biopsy,' Bella pointed out. 'It's not as if they can keep someone under anaesthetic for hours and hours waiting for a result. You had no choice – you had to get Dr Blackman to Emergency. You probably saved his life. He is okay, isn't he?'

Kate's nod was almost distracted. 'They got him up to the cath lab. He had his artery opened with a stent within a couple of hours. They say there's minimal damage and he could be back on deck in a week or so.'

She sighed. 'They did say he's very lucky. He had an episode of VT just after I left, which could easily have been an arrest if he hadn't been in the right place.'

'There you go, then.'

Kate shook her head. 'You don't understand, Bella. It was a catastrophic error. A girl almost lost her leg unnecessarily. If that had happened, my career would have been over. Probably Connor's career as well. How could anyone live with themselves if they made that kind of mistake?'

'But it didn't happen.' Bella closed her eyes. 'Thank goodness.'

Something in her tone made Kate stop pacing for a moment. 'You were up there this afternoon, weren't you? Did you hear something?'

'It was all anyone wanted to talk about.' She smiled at Kate. 'Apparently you bursting into the theatre like that was the most exciting thing that's ever happened up there. Someone said you should have been riding a white charger, dashing in to the rescue.'

It was Kate's turn to close her eyes. She would never forget the look that Connor had given her as he'd stood there with a scalpel in his hand. She'd had no idea whether or not she was too late and the shocked silence around her had suggested that she was.

Kate had never felt more out of control of anything in her

adult life. As if she was clinging to a clifftop by only her fingernails.

'There's been a mistake,' she'd heard herself gasp. 'A mix-up with the slides.' She had been so out of breath, her voice had been no more than an agonised gasp. She'd had to press her hands against her ribs because her chest was hurting so badly.

'The tumour isn't malignant.' Kate had had to drag in some more oxygen. It had sounded horribly like a sob. 'It's a benign osteoid osteoma.'

Another silence. Even more shocked as everybody had realised what could have just taken place. Then Kate had felt the wave of horror that the pathology department – *her* department – could have got something so horribly wrong. And all she'd been able to do was stand there, her breathing still so rough it had sounded like that of a sobbing child.

'Thank you, Dr Graham,' was all Connor had said. 'Now please leave the theatre.'

It hadn't been till hours later that Kate learned that she'd been in time and the girl, Estelle, had not lost her leg. The tension she was under barely lessened, however. She was waiting for Connor to come storming into her department. His fury would be more than justified. The chain of formal complaint, a hearing in front of disciplinary committee and all the repercussions would be equally justified. It was a disaster that Kate had never envisioned herself having to face and she had no idea how to deal with it.

But nothing happened and Kate was confused. She went to visit Lewis but he was recovering from his procedure and the last thing Kate wanted to do was give him the stress of knowing what had happened in the department in his absence. Leaving the coronary care unit, Kate stood for some time in front of the lifts, considering the option of going to find Connor and getting it over with.

But she couldn't quite find the courage and while she was standing there, Bella texted to say she was cooking dinner tonight and suddenly the only place Kate wanted to be was in her own home.

Her refuge.

'Did you see Connor while you were in the theatre suite?'

Bella shook her head. Her face folded into lines of sympathy. 'I did hear that he was absolutely furious. Nobody had ever seen him look the way he did when he came out of Theatre.'

'I don't blame him in the least,' Kate said quietly. 'I should have gone to talk to him but I was...'

Her words trailed away so that she was virtually talking to herself, but she could still hear the trace of astonishment in her tone.

'I was too scared.'

* * *

Bella hadn't seen Kate look this miserable – frightened, even – since... well, not since her young aunt had unexpectedly arrived to join her own family and that had been twenty years ago, so she couldn't really trust the memory, could she?

Yes. She could. She may have only been a small child but she'd recognised the kind of sadness that was the aftermath of something really bad happening. Not that she'd ever found out what had happened that had resulted in Kate ending up on their doorstep to stay forever with her whole life contained in one small suitcase, but she'd instinctively known how lost and lonely the older girl was feeling.

That was why she'd followed her when she'd taken off that

first day. All the way to that junk shop where she'd found Kate clutching the rusty old iron key she'd discovered in a drawer full of ancient cutlery. Bella had tiptoed up to Kate and slipped her small hand into the larger one.

'Come home,' she'd whispered. 'We want you.'

'Keep the key if you want,' the owner of the shop had said. 'It's not worth anything.'

It had been worth something to Kate, though.

Bella's mother, Jackie, had been puzzled by the odd marks on Kate's bedding when she'd gone to change the sheets later that week, but Bella had known what they were. Traces of rust from where the key had been secreted under her pillow at night.

Kate still collected keys. Gorgeous, antique specimens that had come from her travels. A vast old iron one from a castle in Germany. A French one with an intricately curled decorative head. Many, many others. Some were polished brass and some were iron. None of them were rusty, though. Bella could be sure that the original key was still in the collection but it had been restored to its original condition at some point. And kept and treasured.

Had that first key represented escape? Or the determination to lock up the past and move on? Bella had never asked. She'd never needed to. The bond that had been forged that day when she'd taken Kate's hand and led her back to a home where she had been welcomed and loved had been deeper than any words, and it had grown over the years.

Bella often felt lazy and messy and totally without a really worthwhile ambition in her life when she was in Kate's company, but she adored her aunt and she hated seeing her like this again. It was so out of character to see her looking frightened. Disconcerting. As though the world had tilted a little on its axis.

'It'll be okay,' she offered. 'Everybody knows you're brilliant and you couldn't possibly be responsible for a mistake like this. You'll be the head of that department before long.'

Kate's huff of expelled breath was disparaging but it was true. She was brilliant. And totally in control of everything that happened around her. She had taken control of her life from the moment she'd arrived to live with Bella and her family. She'd gone to a new school and achieved academic excellence. She'd gone on to train as a nurse and had come top of her class. Nothing and nobody was allowed to stand in her way. She was fiercely independent and utterly determined and Bella knew that the only sure-fire way to get on the wrong side of Kate was to tell her what to do, especially if Kate knew there was a better way.

Heavens, that was why she'd ended up doing a medical degree in the first place. Too many doctors had told her what to do. Kate was destined to be at the top of a power chain, and she was absolutely the right person to be there. Bella might not be able to understand that drive to be the best and achieve the highest possible standard in everything she did, but she could certainly admire it.

'I'm so proud of you, you know,' she said aloud. 'This wasn't your mistake, and you fixed it, but you're still prepared to take the blame. You really care, about the people who work for you and with you and for the people you do the work for... The patients you never even get to meet.'

They were both silent for a minute. Was Kate also thinking about the teenage girl she'd never met who'd been the patient today? And that Connor had been the girl's surgeon?

That sucked. Bella had watched that chemistry happening

on the dance floor last week and had been secretly thrilled. Kate might be fiercely independent and appear not to need a man in her life on a permanent basis, but everybody needed to be loved, didn't they?

To love someone else?

Okay, she knew how much Kate loved her, but that wasn't enough. For either of them. Especially if Bella was heading for the other side of the world. She might be gone for years and she didn't want to have to worry about Kate being lonely.

And Connor was cute. She instinctively knew she was too young or ditzy or something to be of any interest to him, but she could appreciate his attributes. Not just his looks but that laid-back confidence he had. That almost naughty streak. He was a bit of a renegade was Dr Matthews. A modern-day, professional kind of pirate.

Bella was watching Kate pacing again. She had changed into her jeans but hadn't undone the tight braid her hair was bound up in. Her movements were graceful but... fierce somehow. Like a wild cat prowling the perimeter of its cage.

Why on earth had she been harbouring the hope that the two of them would get together? They were total opposites.

Maybe that was why. Maybe someone like Connor was exactly what Kate needed to balance her. To put some joy into that precisely ordered world that Kate had created for herself. But why would Connor be attracted to someone who was as uptight as Kate? As much as she loved her, Bella couldn't deny that her aunt was a control freak. And maybe too much of a feminist or something because she'd never had a high opinion about the male of the species.

Bella sighed. It had never been likely to happen. And, after today, the chances were probably well below zero.

The sound of the doorbell made them both jump. The two women stared at each other.

'No,' Kate whispered, looking horrified. 'It couldn't be. Could it?'

Bella swallowed hard. It was just the sort of thing Connor would do, wasn't it? To chase someone that he considered had done him harm and sort it out himself, even if it was completely outside any accepted protocol?

The doorbell sounded for the second time. A long, demanding blast.

Bella cleared her throat as she uncurled her legs from the sofa.

'Do you want me to go and see?'

'No.' Kate sucked in an audibly deep, if shaky, breath. 'I'll go.'

* * *

Connor's finger actually hurt because he'd pushed the damn doorbell so hard.

He knew full well he shouldn't be here but Kate hadn't been in her department when he'd finally calmed down enough to be prepared to face the issue, having gathered all the information he could about the day's events. How dared she simply walk off and go home as though nothing untoward had happened today?

Well, he was going to let her know in no uncertain terms just what the implications were of the error that had been made. He could have gone straight to the highest authority that governed the behaviour of physicians within the hospital system, but he was too involved at a personal level here. He'd file a request for disciplinary action when he could be sure he could present it on a professional more than a personal level.

But, dammit, it was one of his patients that it had happened to.

Okay, it hadn't exactly been Kate's fault. He knew about the disruption caused by that fire alarm. He knew that the department had been overloaded with work that included a tutorial taking place and more than one urgent case from Theatre being delivered.

He could also be perfectly confident that Lewis Blackman and Kate would have had it all sorted in no time flat if Lewis hadn't had the misfortune of choosing that moment to have a heart attack.

But...

About to push the doorbell for the third time, Connor found his finger hovering.

But Kate had been the one to find the error, hadn't she? She'd run up to Theatre so fast that she had barely been able to talk through her breathlessness. He'd heard that phone ringing faintly in the technician's room. He could have sent someone to answer it and had the news of the error well before he'd picked up the scalpel.

It wasn't as if he'd even started extending the opening in Estelle's leg. She would be left with barely more than the scar she would have had anyway from the biopsy and fracture repair, even after dealing with the benign tumour.

She had kept her leg. No harm had been done.

Thanks to Kate.

Connor's anger couldn't evaporate instantly but it was diluted with confusion now. He was trying to catch a coherent thought as the door opened in front of him. He found himself staring at Kate.

He could see her fear.

Not the same kind of fear he'd seen that night on the dance floor but it was close enough. And this time he could also see the determination to face whatever was coming. Kate wasn't going to turn and run away.

Not this time.

But how could he yell at her? Something was swimming up through his brain. If he did that, it would only justify the way she'd reacted the other night. Give her a reason to lump him in with whatever brute of a male had done her emotional harm in the past. For some inexplicable reason, it suddenly seemed very important that he didn't give her the opportunity to do that.

And what on earth would be the point of venting his anger by attacking Kate anyway?

He should be thanking her.

She was waiting for him to yell at her. Seconds ticked past as they stared at each other and she was starting to look as confused as Connor was feeling.

* * *

The anger was there.

Kate could see it. Feel it, even, like a curious humming in the air between them. She fully expected to get the brunt of his fury, and fair enough. She deserved it. She couldn't even blame him for breaking unspoken rules and coming into her private life to do so. She deserved this as well because she'd been too much of a coward to go and see him in their professional arena.

She straightened her back and steeled herself to deal with whatever was coming. She couldn't fight back. Not this time.

Except... Connor said nothing. He was looking at her as though he'd forgotten what it was he had planned to say.

Even more oddly, that humming sensation had changed. It was still there but she couldn't attribute it to anger. It was too soft now. Too...

Kate didn't know what it was. And she didn't know what to say to this man on her doorstep. He wasn't even looking angry any longer and it was confusing, that's what it was. Anger she could handle. She knew exactly how to distance herself and raise impenetrable barriers to protect the parts of her that had nothing to do with her work. The lessons had been unbearable at the time but they had stood her in very good stead ever since. But those skills seemed to be redundant.

Why had Connor come here if he didn't want to tear strips off her for the incompetence of her department?

Why was he here at all when he could have simply gone and filed a demand for a disciplinary hearing of some kind?

'Kate?' The voice came from behind her. 'Is everything okay?'

Connor seemed to be collecting himself as Bella pressed close to Kate's side.

'Everything's fine,' he said.

Kate could feel her jaw dropping. What on earth was going on here?

'I came to collect Kate,' Connor was saying to Bella. 'There's something I think she needs to see.'

Collect her? Did he think he could just turn up and order her to accompany him to God knows where? Well... Connor Matthews had a few things he needed to learn about her, didn't he? Kate didn't take direct orders from anyone. Especially not from a physical hulk that exuded pure masculinity.

Connor's gaze swung back to meet hers and Kate was astonished to see the confusion in his eyes. As though he had no idea what he was doing or why he was doing it. It was in that moment that Kate realised he had come here with the intention of tearing strips off her, but something had made him change his mind. And maybe he was still trying to work out whatever it was himself.

'I'd like to take you there,' he said slowly. 'If that's all right with you?'

Bella was eyeing the helmet dangling from Connor's hand. 'On your bike? Cool!'

A crisp nod from Connor. 'I have a spare helmet on the bike.'

Bella was eyeing Connor now. Then she looked at Kate. 'You should go,' she said. 'Dinner's going to be ages cos I forgot to turn the oven on when I put the chicken in.'

Kate barely heard what Bella was saying.

If he'd commanded her to go with him it would have been easy to refuse. She wouldn't have been able to do anything else. But he was asking and there was a plea amongst that confusion in his eyes. As if he needed her help to sort out what was going on in his head.

Where did Connor want to take her? And *why*?

Getting on the back on this man's motorbike would have been unthinkable even yesterday but suddenly it was a minor detail in whatever else was going on.

Kate had no idea at all what it was all about but, astonishingly, amidst the emotional turmoil of this whole day and the confusion it was ending in was a feeling that this was, in some way, very simple.

Going off to some unknown destination with Connor, on the back of his bike, felt... right.

Her nod was as crisp as his had been. 'I'll just fetch a jacket.'

* * *

They left the city and headed west.

Kate had never been on a motorbike before. At first it was terrifying. All she could think of was how little protection they had between their bodies and the other vehicles around them. Then she was far too conscious of the black tarmac beneath them that was going past so fast she couldn't even count the broken white lines that marked the centre of the open road they were soon on. She could feel the wind whipping the parts of her body that were exposed.

And the part that wasn't? Well… that was in close contact with Connor's body. Her arms were around his waist, hanging on for dear life. There was a thick layer of clothing and leather between her breasts and Connor's back, but she could swear she was aware of his warmth and she was grateful for how solid he felt as the reality around them passed in a blur.

The ride seemed to go on for a very long time and slowly Kate could feel her terror ebbing. She could feel how relaxed Connor was as he tilted when they cornered and she could sense how responsive and powerful the motorbike was. A trickle of something like excitement bubbled up inside her. She – Kate Graham – was doing this. Riding at high speed on a motorbike. Doing something daring. Different.

Getting a life?

It was then that Kate began to take some notice of her surroundings, and she finally realised where they were heading. As the brightness of a late summer's day began to fade into dusk, they were getting closer and closer to one of New Zealand's most famous beaches.

Piha.

Famed for its scenic beauty and great surf. That it could be a dangerous beach to swim at didn't deter many thousands of people from visiting this beach at regular intervals but, despite having been within its reach her whole life, Kate had never set foot on the black iron sands.

The sand glistened in the evening sunlight with the tide well out. There were really two beaches here, the north and south stretches, divided by an ancient formation known as Lion Rock because it looked like a lion resting on the sand. Kate recognised the famous rock instantly as Connor took the bike down the access road. She still had no idea why Connor had brought her here and she definitely didn't expect to have to climb the rock, but apparently it was important.

'We'll have to hurry,' Connor said apologetically. 'Or we'll be too late. Are you up for it?'

Kate took in a good lungful of the wonderful sea air. 'Bring it on.'

Connor set a brisk pace across the sand but slowed as they began the track leading up the lion's back. Kate caught the frequent glances that were assessing how fit she was. She must have made the grade because Connor picked up the pace, walking just half a pace ahead of her.

It made her feel good that she could keep up with him. Being so far from the city in such an astonishingly beautiful part of the country should be making her feel even better, but Kate still felt confused about why she was here and there was a nagging sensation that she had backed herself into a corner. They were miles from anywhere. Connor could say anything he wanted and she couldn't even walk away if she didn't like it.

What on earth had she been thinking to put herself into such a vulnerable position?

Connor stopped so abruptly Kate banged into him.

'Sorry.'

'No worries. I shouldn't have stopped like that but this looks like a good spot.' He stepped off the track. 'Be careful. Wouldn't want you slipping.'

No. They weren't that far from the dramatic cliffs that must represent part of the lion's mane when it was viewed from the right direction. It was a spot that gave a great view of the surf below, where a number of surfers were making the most of the last daylight. Connor didn't go far off the track. He chose a smooth rocky area just protruding from the short tussock, dropped his leather jacket that he'd peeled off during the climb up the hill and sat down. Kate sat down on the uphill side of his spot. It made her slightly higher. Maybe it made her feel slightly more in control.

Connor said nothing. He shaded his eyes with his hand and watched the surfers. For a long moment Kate found herself watching him, still wondering what the purpose of this expedition was.

He looked tired, she decided. His face was very still and his jaw looked dark with a day's growth of beard. He'd been wearing a black T-shirt under the leather jacket and it left his arms bare. She could see the curve of his muscles just under the sleeves and the skin looked so smooth. Free of the dark scatter of hair on his forearms.

The hand that wasn't shielding his eyes from the glare of the lowering sun was resting on the thigh closest to Kate. A large hand but the fingers were long and beautifully defined. A powerful but clever hand. Kate couldn't help remembering what that hand had felt like on her back, guiding her expertly though complicated dance moves.

With a jerk of effort she lifted her gaze and managed to focus on the expanse of the beach and the surrounding hills. After another long moment Kate found herself also watching the activity in the surf far below.

The surfers sat on their boards, riding the swells beyond where the waves were breaking. Time and again they let waves go by that looked huge to Kate. She didn't understand what they were waiting for but then a wave came that was better in some way and there was frantic movement as the riders paddled furiously to position themselves and stand up on their boards.

And then it was a joy to watch as they skimmed sideways along the wall of water, being chased by the curling lip of the breaking wave. The sky behind them was changing colour and a faint pink tinge began to strengthen and take on streaks of yellow and orange brilliance. Several surfers headed for the shore but one was still out there and produced the longest ride Kate had seen. Not only that, they were also treated to a show of talent with the rider doing some spectacular turns and a final flip that had him airborne against the glow of the sunset.

'*Wow*,' Kate breathed. 'Did you see that?'

'How good would it feel,' Connor murmured, 'to be able to do that?'

'It must feel a bit like flying,' Kate suggested.

'Or dancing,' Connor said quietly.

His gaze met hers and Kate felt the solid ground she was sitting on simply vanish. She was hanging in space. Falling...

Had she really been afraid of Connor wanting to talk about what had happened at work today?

It paled in comparison to talking about what had happened between them on the dance floor.

Why hadn't it occurred to Kate that, in order for herself to have felt that way, it had to be coming, at least in part, from Connor feeling the same way?

Oh... Lord...

That connection was there again. She was falling into his eyes.

Falling in love?

No. That couldn't happen. Kate couldn't even try going there, and if Connor knew what was good for him, he wouldn't want to go there either.

But maybe Connor didn't know what was good for him.

'Kate...'

He seemed to be asking her permission to continue. Her name hung in the air, a low, sexy rumble.

She couldn't respond. It was hard enough to take a breath. She had to close her eyes to make the effort.

And when she opened them again, Connor's brow was creased in a frown. He turned away to stare down at the sunset-gilded surf and Kate could hear him taking a deep, deep breath as though trying to centre himself.

* * *

What the hell had happened there?

That feeling...

Kind of the same as he'd felt dancing with Kate that night. He hadn't expected it to happen again. Wasn't ready for it because he still had no idea what it meant.

His gaze slid sideways again involuntarily.

The bike ride had considerably messed with Kate's hair. The plait was still there but it had come undone and was now hanging over her shoulder. Wisps and even loops of hair had been tugged free as well and they hung like a soft frame around a face flushed with exertion. Maybe it was a trick of the setting sun that made her eyes look so incredibly bright.

Bright enough to blind him?

Why was he so drawn to this woman? Kate was so not his type. She was so prim and proper. Closed off.

Boring.

No. That was the wrong word entirely. How could anyone that seemed to have the ability to completely disrupt his life and mess with his head be considered boring? Not that the disruption was welcome or anything, but it was intriguing. Confusing. It needed sorting out.

Connor sighed. That wasn't the reason he'd brought her here. Not that he'd known what the reason for this impulsive journey had been when he'd instigated it. He hadn't even known during the ride or the climb up this hill, but he knew now. He turned his gaze back to the waves beneath them.

'Estelle Montgomery has a passion for surfing,' he told Kate quietly. 'She won a junior section of a championship a couple of years ago. She's quite confident that she can win more. She wants to represent Northland in national events. Her dream is to represent New Zealand in an international competition.'

He glanced at Kate again.

She was staring down at the sea, watching the lone surfer who was finally calling it a day and riding the dregs of a wave back to shore. Was she remembering the thrilling last ride of the day that they'd just watched? Imagining it to be Estelle, like he had?

Realising what it would have meant to the young girl if she had lost her leg?

Kate seemed to feel the intensity of his gaze. She turned her head slowly and the instant her eyes met his, Connor knew that she got it.

All of it.

His smile felt crooked. 'Life's full of corners, isn't it? They appear from nowhere and sometimes you have no control over which ones you have to take.'

Kate was silent. She held his gaze.

'One wrong turn can be enough to change the whole direction of your life and often, no matter how badly you might want it, you can't find a way back.'

Connor was silent for a moment.

'A terrible mistake almost happened today. A corner could have been turned that would have changed a great many lives, but most of all Estelle's.'

Kate wasn't looking at him now. Her head was bowed.

'You saved more than Estelle's leg today,' Connor told her softly. 'You saved her dreams and they're what make life worth living, aren't they?'

* * *

Kate couldn't answer.

Connor's words had slipped into a place they shouldn't have been allowed to enter. The sentiment they expressed was touching a place so deep and so raw it felt as if it was bleeding despite the touch being so gentle.

He had a wisdom she had not expected.

And a depth of caring for a single patient that blew her away.

Kate knew all about those corners in life. Obviously, Connor did too. What turning points had he been forced to follow in his life? Was he trying to find his way back? She certainly wasn't but if none of it had ever happened, what would her life be like now?

How would she feel if she'd had an upbringing like Bella's, for instance, and was now sitting here with Connor Matthews?

She'd feel full of hope. She would know that she was on the verge of falling in love with a very special man.

She would have dreams for her future that were nothing like any dreams she currently held.

There would be a very big corner to turn in her life that she would take with joy and the absolute conviction that it was the best possible direction to take.

But there was no such corner in the road map of Kate's life. Or, if there was, it was blocked by a barrier she had no idea how to negotiate.

And that was indescribably sad.

Sad enough to give her a tightness in her chest that squeezed and squeezed until it rose up into her throat and passed the back of her nose to reach her eyes. Tight enough to squeeze a single tear from them.

Unbelievable.

Kate hadn't cried since she was fifteen years old.

'We'd better go,' she heard Connor say. 'Let's get off this hill before it's too dark to see anything.'

Kate nodded, surreptitiously wiping those errant drops of moisture away before following Connor's example and scrambling to her feet. She was glad it was getting dark so quickly now. At least Connor couldn't possibly see that she'd been crying.

'Ready?' Connor held out his hand to help her over some small rocks to get to the smoother surface of the track. Without thinking, Kate accepted the offer.

'I'm ready,' she agreed. 'Let's go.'

* * *

A tiny catch in her voice made Connor stop.

He was still holding her hand and he was standing with his back to the sea. The last rays of the sun before it dipped below the horizon were doing their best to outshine and out-colour anything that had gone before. The light was so bright behind him that he was probably no more than a dark blob for Kate, but he could see her face with the utmost clarity. He could see the tangle of her dark lashes where moisture still clung.

Good grief... she'd been *crying*?

The woman who was so tightly walled off from the world around her that she'd earned the reputation of being an ice queen had been moved to tears. By what? Estelle's story?

A reminder of some trauma in her own past?

It didn't matter. Connor knew he was seeing the real person here. The Kate who could dance like a dream. Who could care enough to cry. He also knew that he was seeing something that very few – if any – other people got to see.

A tight feeling in his chest expanded so suddenly it seemed to explode with a curious mix of warmth and... longing.

For what, Connor didn't know. What he did know was that he had to pull Kate closer. He heard himself sigh as he did so. A sound of surrender that ended in the whisper of her name.

And then he kissed her.

6

The feeling of falling reached an unbearable intensity.

Maybe it was the glow of the glorious sunset. Or perhaps the emotions that Connor's words had stirred up. Whatever the cause, there was no way of catching herself in time and, for a few memorable seconds when his lips touched hers, Kate simply let herself go.

She fell into the softness of his lips and the warmth of his body as he drew her close. The knot of longing deep in her belly spiralled into a white-hot glow. Kate felt her lips parting beneath Connor's, but it was in that split second before his tongue touched hers that she realised just how far out of control this was.

With a gasp, she put her hands on Connor's chest and pushed herself away.

They stood there, staring at each other.

'We – we need to go,' Kate stammered. 'It's really getting dark now.'

'Hmm.' Connor licked his lips and Kate felt an odd melting sensation in the core of her body, but he didn't say anything else. He reached for her hand again and this time they reached the track.

He held her hand until they came to a narrow section of steps where they needed to go in single file and by the time they reached the sand, they were walking side by side, the same way they had done when they had arrived.

They still hadn't said anything. That kiss hung between them. An invitation or a solid wall?

Something had to be said. How could Kate climb onto the back of that bike and hang on to Connor for as long as it would take for him to deliver her back home if she had to wonder whether he saw this as the start of a relationship? If he was taking it for granted that it would follow the usual path and she would be panting to get into his bed in no time flat, like she could imagine any other woman he dated would be?

What if it got that far and he ended up being... disappointed? Disgusted, even?

Kate didn't want that to happen. There was something between them that had become so much bigger this evening. Something that was too precious to risk.

She opened her mouth. 'I'm not looking for a relationship, Connor.'

'Okay.'

Oh, God... Was that *relief* in his tone?

For some reason that hurt rather a lot.

'I'd like us to be friends, though,' she added. 'If that's possible.'

'Anything's possible,' Connor said, sounding neutral now. They reached the spot where he'd parked the bike and he handed Kate her helmet. In the deepening twilight she saw the gleam of teeth as he smiled.

'I like you, Kate,' he said. His smile widened. 'I'm not sure exactly why but you...' His voice faded, giving his last words a sincerity that took Kate's breath away. 'You're... special. You surprise me.'

Kate had to swallow a small but very unexpected lump in her throat. 'You surprise me, too.'

'Do I?' Connor zipped up his jacket. 'How so?'

'Well... I expected you to rake me over the coals over what happened today. You had – you still have – every right to.'

Connor shrugged. 'I suspect you've been doing that to yourself.'

Kate bit her lip. 'What are you going to do about it?'

'What would you do?'

'Probably take the matter to a disciplinary committee,' Kate admitted.

Connor rammed his helmet onto his head and lowered the visor. He looked far more menacing now. Big and dark and... threatening.

'There's another way of looking at it,' he suggested.

'Which is?'

'It could be a good platform to use to make a case for getting that mini pathology lab set up in the theatre suite as soon as possible. We've been trying to get it established for years and the powers-that-be keep stalling. What happened today could be seen as being more about the way the whole system is failing its patients than trying to make it the fault of an individual. I'm not saying that your registrar doesn't need a bit of up-skilling but it would be good to see something positive come out of it, wouldn't it?'

'Oh... yes...' How many times was her breath going to be stolen tonight?

First by the depth of involvement and caring this man had for his patients and then by that kiss, and now by the way he could not only let go of an entirely justifiable anger but do a complete U-turn and go in a new direction.

An excellent direction.

'I could help,' Kate offered. 'I could do some research and compile a list of cases where the time taken to do biopsies could have had a bearing in the patient's outcome.'

'Cool.' Connor swung his leg over the bike and kicked it into life. 'We'll talk.'

Kate climbed on behind him. She raised her voice. 'If Bella's actually remembered to turn the oven on, there might be a roast chicken waiting. You could stay for dinner and we could talk about it.'

* * *

They not only talked about it; they came up with a plan of action that they got stuck into the very next day by going to see the clinical director of St Patrick's hospital.

'If nothing else,' Kate finished their presentation by saying, 'if news of this near-miss got into the media, it would be a good thing to be able to say that definitive steps were being taken to make sure it never happened again.'

Connor was impressed by her inspired addition. The clinical director looked thoughtful.

'I still need the facts and figures to take to the funding committee. How soon can you present a report?'

Connor sounded confident. 'The end of the week. Early next week at the latest.' He glanced at Kate for confirmation, and she nodded.

The clinical director looked from Connor to Kate and back again. He shook his head and actually smiled.

'I think it might work,' he said, 'but I have to say you two seem like a very unlikely team.'

Unlikely they may be but it became clear rapidly that they worked very well together. Connor spent more than one evening in the pathology department helping Kate locate and document cases. Not that they needed anything more than Estelle's case but it wouldn't hurt to strengthen it.

'How's Estelle doing?' Kate asked.

'Great. She's up and around on her crutches. I'll let her go home very soon.'

'How long before she can go surfing again?'

'I'm not sure I'm going to be able to control that one. I suspect she'll be in the water as soon as that fracture's healed. I'll keep a close watch on her for the next few years, though, to make sure she doesn't get a recurrence.'

Kate smiled at him.

'What?'

'Nothing... I was just imagining you keeping a watch on her by going to some surfing competition.'

Connor grinned. 'I might just do that. Want to come with me?'

The question hung in the air. They were talking about the future here. Possibly a long time into the future. Would they still be friends?

Connor hoped so.

More than friends?

No. Kate had made it clear she didn't want a relationship. And he didn't either. Not with someone like Kate, anyway. She was so different from the usual type of women he had enjoyed brief relationships with that he wouldn't know where to start. And if you did start, how on earth would you finish? Finishing always had to be on the agenda. It wasn't fair to expect anyone to want to stay with him long term. Not when he couldn't offer what it was that women always wanted. Even a friendship with this woman was not something to be taken lightly.

It felt like a privilege.

Connor insisted on walking Kate back to the car-parking building when they finished those sessions late at night. Offering protection to a woman was mandatory in his book.

'You just never know,' he said, overriding her protests sternly.

His point was proven on that last night, when they'd been putting the finishing touches to their report. He'd seen Kate to her car and was heading for his bike when he heard the voices behind him. Turning, he saw that a man was approaching Kate so Connor headed over as well.

The man's voice was raised by the time he got close.

'I just want change so I can get a parking ticket from the damned machine,' he was shouting angrily. 'You're a doctor, for God's sake... it's not as if it's a big deal.'

Connor was close enough now to smell the alcohol fumes coming from the man, who was wearing a very scruffy overcoat despite the fact that it was a warm evening. He was also carrying a plastic shopping bag that appeared to be stuffed full of old clothing. Was he homeless? Had he found a good way of conning small change out of a large number of people? Whatever. He wasn't a small man and Kate wasn't looking happy.

In fact, when Connor stepped in to stand beside her, his shoulder touched hers and he could actually feel how tense her whole body was.

Kate was frightened and Connor suddenly felt very angry.

'Get lost,' he told the man. 'And if I find you here again, intimidating women, I'll call Security. No... I might just deliver you to the nearest police station myself.'

'Oh... yeah?' The man swayed slightly and then took a closer look at Connor and backed away. 'I only wanted a couple of dollars,' he muttered.

'He would probably have just gone away if you'd given him something,' Connor reassured Kate. 'I don't think he intended you any real harm.'

'No.' But Kate seemed frozen to the spot.

'Not that I'm saying you *should* have given him the money,' Connor added. He'd known instinctively the first time he'd met Kate that the worst way to gain her cooperation would be by making demands. She needed to be treated with respect. She *deserved* to be treated with respect, dammit.

But even so, there was something strange about the way she was standing, holding herself so rigidly. Connor put his arm around her shoulders.

'It's okay,' he said. 'He's gone.'

She flinched at his touch. He felt it and a chill ran down Connor's spine, but instead of letting go he turned Kate to face him, holding both her shoulders.

'What is it, Katie?' he asked softly. 'What happened to you? Did someone hurt you?'

She didn't have to confirm what he suspected. Connor had no difficulty putting two and two together. The way she'd looked at him that night of the fancy-dress ball. The way she kept herself socially aloof. The knowledge that there was a sensual woman hidden – *protected* – under that prim exterior.

'Who was it?' A burn of an anger like Connor had never felt before ignited in his gut. 'Who hurt you?'

There was a desperate look in her eyes. As though she was ashamed that anyone knew. As if she thought that somehow it had been her fault.

It had to have been a man.

'Your father?' he ground out. 'A boyfriend?'

A reluctant nod. A pause and then a firmer movement of her head.

'My father was... an alcoholic,' Kate said quietly. 'That man smelled...'

'I know.' Connor pulled her closer so that he could hold her. Protect her. And he had the feeling that he hadn't heard the whole story by any means.

'And the boyfriend?'

He got no answer but he felt the way Kate shrank in his arms.

'Oh, my God...' he murmured. 'He hit you?'

Kate tried to pull away. Connor didn't know whether continuing to hold her would make it worse but he couldn't help himself. He wasn't that man. He'd earned her trust by now, hadn't he?

He was certainly about to find out.

'You're safe, Katie,' he said. 'I'm not going to hurt you. I could never hurt you. You trust me... don't you?'

She was still rigid, poised to struggle and flee. Time froze for a heartbeat and then another and then Connor felt the fight drain out of her body. She almost sagged against him.

'Yes,' she whispered. 'I do trust you.'

Connor ended up sitting in the car with her that night and they talked for a long time before Kate drove herself home. She made him promise never to tell anybody what he'd learned about her.

'Especially Bella,' she warned. 'She's never known the real reason I went to live with my brother. I think she's guessed that David and I grew up in an abusive household but I've never told anyone how bad it really was.'

Connor had to unclench his fists. He could join more dots

together now. No wonder Kate wasn't into the idea of having a relationship. The kind of damage that could be done with a history like hers was unimaginable.

Even if she wanted a relationship or had wanted one in the past, it would take a very strong man to be able to get past that kind of damage.

And yet that was what made Kate who she was, wasn't it?

Unique.

And he wasn't exactly without emotional baggage himself. Maybe this gave them more in common than she realised.

Maybe he could help Kate.

Fix her, even?

Tread carefully, he warned himself. *Someone could get hurt.*

Someone like Kate.

* * *

'Have you been to bed with him yet?'

'*Bella*!' Kate shook her head. 'I really shouldn't let you have wine with dinner, should I?'

Bella tossed her head, unrepentant. She eyed Kate. 'You haven't, have you?'

'We're friends, that's all.'

Bella snorted. 'Don't give me that. You're besotted with each other. You've been having coffee dates and dinner dates for weeks now. You had all those late nights closeted in the pathology department working on that report thing. He must have kissed you by now.'

The heat that infused Kate's cheeks came from nowhere and startled both of them.

'You're *blushing*.' Bella's astonishment became laughter. 'Auntie Katie blushing. Who knew?'

'Give it a rest, Bella. This thing between Connor and me is friendship, that's all.'

A friendship like nothing Kate had ever had in her life. It had begun with that bike ride to the beach and that gentle kiss in the sunset.

No. It had really begun that night on the dance floor, hadn't it?

Or maybe even when she'd followed those tyre tracks to where he'd wheeled that ridiculous machine into the children's ward.

It had been strengthened by the addition of trust in the way Connor had handled the incident of the diagnostic error with Estelle's tumour. Their dinner date this week had been a celebration of the approval for immediate funding of the pathology lab in Theatre. Within a short space of time, hopefully, Kate was to have the honour of being the first pathologist to be on duty for Theatre, to have a test run to check that they had all the equipment they needed in the sparkling new designated area. It might be no more than the size of a cupboard, sheared off from one end of the staffroom with a sliding glass hatch into one of the operating theatres, but it was a huge step for all the interested parties and Kate was as excited about it as Connor.

What had taken their friendship to a completely new level, however, was that incident in the car park.

Connor was the first person she had ever told about her past. Even the men she'd had relationships with in the last few years had never known.

Could that be part of the reason why they'd never worked out?

And while Kate might protest that it was nothing more than friendship with Connor, she knew it was more than that. Or potentially more than that. On both sides? They seemed to be in a kind of holding pattern. Spending time together and keeping options open without taking things any further.

Did Connor want to?

Did she want to or was it just that she was reluctant to lose this amazing connection that they seemed to have? And she would lose it, if Connor learned about the parts of her story that she still had locked away.

'It's not going anywhere,' she told her niece firmly. 'So stop going on about it.'

But Bella couldn't let it go. She refilled both their wine glasses. Kate tried to refuse. She started gathering the dishes that should have been loaded into the dishwasher long ago.

'Leave it.' The very idea of ordering Kate around made Bella offer up a surprisingly contrite smile. 'Please? I really like talking to you.'

Kate liked it too. She hadn't realised how nice it would be to have company in her home at night. Someone to share food with. Even if they were both busy with other things in the evenings it was nice to have someone else in the house. To not feel so... alone.

'Just don't go on about Connor, then,' she relented.

Bella sighed theatrically. 'But he's gorgeous. You're both single. You like each other. I can't see what the problem is.'

'Neither of us wants a long-term relationship.'

'So have a short-term one, then. A friendship with benefits.' Bella's eyebrows wiggled suggestively. 'Some *fun*. I'll bet Connor would be up for it.'

'I'll bet.' Kate's tone was dry. 'And that's one of the reasons it couldn't possibly work. He's got a reputation for breaking hearts. He's probably the world's expert in "friendships with benefits". What woman in her right mind would want to be another notch on someone's bedpost?'

'He's only like that because he hasn't found the right woman. That might be you.'

Oh... She had to stop this conversation. That feeling of wanting... hoping... was too painful.

She gave her head a sharp shake. 'I don't do casual sex.'

The odd look that Bella had on her face made Kate sigh. 'So you've heard the rumours, then.'

Bella chewed her bottom lip and wouldn't meet Kate's eyes.

'I'm not a middle-aged virgin and I'm not a lesbian, okay? People round St Pat's have short memories. You met Tim, didn't you? That nephrologist I was with for two years?'

Bella nodded. 'Seems a long time ago.'

It was. Over three years, in fact. Tim had left St Pat's not long after the relationship had ended. Connor had arrived not long after that. Hospitals were like that. People coming and going all the time. Romances starting. Others ending.

'He was a nice guy,' Bella added. 'What went wrong, Kate?'

Kate shrugged. 'He wanted a family. I didn't.'

And Tim had pushed and made her realise how impossible it would be to ever go there again. So she had pushed back and the distance created so swiftly had made it obvious that there hadn't been enough there in the first place.

Bella's bewilderment was written all over her face. 'It's all I want,' she said. 'Is that wrong – to want a husband and a bunch of kids and not be bothered about much else?'

'It's not wrong. It's who you are.' Kate smiled. 'And I'm sure you'll get exactly what you want. You'll probably have three kids by the time you're my age. Good grief, that'll make me, what – a great-aunt?'

'You'll be a famous pathologist great-aunt. I'll bring all the kids to visit and they'll drive you crazy, making a mess all over the place.'

'Hey, I got used to that living with you lot.'

Kate was more shocked than she was prepared to admit at the thought of being part of an older generation. It felt like something very important was passing her by. That she'd end up having regrets. She shook the thought away.

'Why don't we ring home?' she suggested. 'And see what they're all doing?'

Bella let Kate make the call.

Clearly one of the twins was at home and answered the phone because Kate was laughing in no time flat and it was quite a while before she even got a word in edgeways.

And then it was her mother's turn, and Kate seemed to be very interested in hearing how her brother was doing. Michael was in his third year of med school now, living a long way from home in Dunedin. Apparently he was also changing flats because Kate went hunting for a pen and paper to take down his new details. She had the phone tucked against her shoulder as she wrote.

Sipping the last of her glass of wine, Bella was content to wait for once because she had a lot to think about.

How embarrassing was it that Kate knew about those rumours? Bella had been horrified when she'd found out from her fellow theatre nurses. She'd taken a great deal of satisfaction in scorching the horrible innuendoes by announcing that her aunt was, in fact, in a relationship with Connor Matthews.

Her colleagues had been more than a bit sceptical, mind you, and Bella couldn't blame them. She'd come to the conclusion that Kate and Connor were an impossible match herself, weeks ago. Just before the man himself had turned up on the doorstep and whisked Kate off on the back of that gorgeous bike. He hadn't brought her home until hours later and there'd been a glow in her eyes that Bella had never seen before.

One that had been there with increasing frequency over the last few weeks, but now Kate was claiming that it was nothing more than a friendship and never would be. And she'd sounded pretty convincing.

Bella could feel herself frowning. It couldn't be allowed to fizzle out like that. Or not get going properly or whatever the problem was. But what could she possibly do about it? She could hear an echo of her mother's voice in her head. Or was it Kate's?

Don't meddle, Bella. You'll only cause trouble.

With a sigh, she tuned back in to the phone conversation.

'Only if he's not busy,' Kate was saying. There was a short silence and then Bella's father must have been given the phone. 'Hi, David.'

Kate was smiling into the phone. 'Yes, I'm good, thanks. Yes...' She was looking at Bella as she listened. 'She's behaving herself. Her cooking's improving, too – when she remembers to turn the oven on.' The chuckle was a happy sound. 'How are things with you?'

Kate's expression changed in the space of a heartbeat. '*What*?' Her voice lowered. '*When*?'

She turned away, leaving Bella to stare at her back, unable to get any clues from her face as to what might be being discussed. It was something that wasn't good, that was for sure.

'I hope you didn't say anything.' Kate listened a little longer and then nodded. 'Well, let's hope that an end to it. Once and for all. Yes... okay... Yes, she's right here.'

Kate was turning back as she spoke. She held the phone out.

'What's going on?' Bella whispered urgently, covering the mouthpiece with her hand. 'What was that all about?'

The head shake was definite. 'Nothing.'

Bella uncovered the mouthpiece cautiously. 'Hello?'

'Bells.' Her father sounded perfectly normal. 'Your mum's waving at me. She wants to know when you're coming down for a visit.'

'Soon. I'll try for my next weekend off if I can get a cheap flight. I'm trying to save my money, you know.'

'We'll spring for the flight,' her father promised. 'Just give us the dates.'

'Hang on.' Bella walked towards the calendar that hung on the kitchen wall, where she'd marked all her days off with a smiley face. She had to go past Kate, who didn't seem to notice. She was sitting at the table, staring into space.

'Hey, it's only two weeks away.'

'Great. Tell Kate we'd love to see her if she wants to come with you.'

Bella turned her head to pass on the invitation. Kate hadn't moved a muscle and she looked… weird.

'She might have better things to do,' she said experimentally. 'She's got a new boyfriend.'

Yup. There was no reaction from Kate at all. She was in another place entirely, staring at nothing at all.

Looking as though she'd seen a ghost.

7

'Where's Dr Graham?'

'In the morgue.' The technician was one of the reduced number of people who worked in the laboratory to do the work that couldn't fit in to the busy day shift. Most of the benches in the area were deserted at the moment and the whirr of electronic machinery was no more than a background hum.

'Is she busy?' Connor knew that Kate was getting involved in the forensic side of pathology. Maybe there'd been a suspicious death that needed urgent investigation.

'Something to do with a research trial. She said she didn't need any help. Go on in. Kate won't mind.' The technician smiled at Connor. 'She might be glad of some company.' The smile turned into a grimace. 'Company that can talk back, anyway.'

Clearly, some of the things that happened in the basement of St Pat's were well out of the comfort zone of this young girl. Autopsies were out of the comfort zone of most people.

Including himself?

Yes. Connor walked slowly through the laboratory to the

back entrance of the morgue, where bodies were stored in their refrigerated cubicles. This wasn't an area he could enter with any great enthusiasm. If he stopped to think about it, it was downright weird that he was drawn to a person that was more than comfortable with it all. Someone who had a passion for it, even.

But drawn he was. The piece of news he had, that the sparkly new microscope had been delivered upstairs, could easily have waited until tomorrow. It could have been passed on with a phone call or an email. But Connor had seen it as a compelling reason to go and see if Kate was still at work and, if she wasn't, he would have headed straight for her house.

And he would have felt surprisingly comfortable turning up unannounced on her doorstep, he realised. Almost as if they were dating. Except they weren't, of course. They'd been spending a lot of time together setting up the mini pathology lab in Theatre. There'd been lots of coffees and even a dinner, but Connor was still treading carefully, at a loss as to precisely what direction he was treading in.

It wasn't heading away from Kate, though, was it?

He walked through the chill of the room where the bodies were stored. Empty to all outward appearances but Connor felt far from alone. He looked through the wide glass window of the partition into the next area.

A body lay exposed on the stainless-steel table in the centre of the room. A middle-aged male with an open chest that suggested the autopsy was well under way. Kate, bent over the body and completely focused on her task, was dressed in what looked like theatre gear with a heavy-duty plastic apron over the gown. The clothing was baggy and made Kate look smaller somehow.

Or was that because she was working alone in a place that

already made Connor feel isolated and uncomfortable? Even from this distance he could sense the clinical detachment with which Kate was working. She had learned how to deal with this environment by closing herself off from reactions that were at an emotional level. She was good at that, wasn't she? A lesson she had probably learned as a child and a big part of who she was. And thank goodness there were people who could do that because this kind of work might be distasteful to many, but it was a vital part of the world of medicine.

'Hey...' He poked his head through the door. 'Is it okay if I come in?'

Kate looked up, surprised. 'Yes, of course.'

'Do I need to put any gear on?'

'Some booties would be good but you don't need anything else, unless you want to get your hands dirty.' She smiled at his expression. 'It's okay, I'm almost done. I won't ask you to help.' She was lifting an organ from the body. The heart. 'This is the bit I was after.'

Connor was already hating the smell but he went closer, following Kate as she took the heart to a set of scales hanging over a bench. His gaze skittered past the body on the table. 'Interesting case?'

'Part of a research trial.' Kate activated a recording device to dictate the weight and external appearance of the organ and then took the heart from the bowl of the scales and laid it on a dissection board that had an impressive array of scalpels and other surgical instruments laid out beside it. 'It's looking at sudden death in patients who are known to have heart failure.'

'How come?'

'Well, it's commonly thought that many of the deaths are due to an irregular heart rhythm that becomes fatal, but it appears that a high percentage – maybe up to 75 per cent – of these people have actually had a heart attack and if that's the case, different drug therapy may well protect them.'

'Hmm. International trial?'

'Yes. They're looking at thousands of cases. I'm going to present data on our contribution in a couple of months' time. In Zurich.'

'Cool.' Connor was watching the meticulous dissection Kate was doing on the coronary arteries of the heart. 'You would have made a great surgeon.'

Kate's smile was crooked. 'Can't kill anyone in here. And... I like working alone.'

She liked being alone. How many people, Connor wondered, had any idea of the 'other' Kate? The secret one that was hidden inside a respected pathologist who would probably be warmly welcomed to present data at an important international conference?

The secret Kate. The imprisoned, sensual Kate.

Connor had a sudden desire to be out on the highway, with the miles peeling away beneath the wheels of his bike. With Kate's arms wrapped around his waist and her hair flying in the wind beneath her helmet.

No. What he wanted was to be somewhere with soft music playing and an empty dance floor so that he could have Kate entirely to himself. Soft lighting, too. Moonlight would be enough.

And then it hit him.

What he actually wanted was more than that. He simply wanted Kate. He wanted to make love to her. Slowly. Deliciously. Probably more than once.

Whoa!

Had any of that shown on his face? Thank goodness Kate was absorbed in her task.

'Look at that.' The hard white shell of a major blood vessel within the heart was opening slowly beneath the tip of a precisely wielded scalpel. The clot was huge and dark and ugly.

'Pretty conclusive evidence.' Kate sounded pleased. 'I might get some photos.' Stripping off her gloves, she walked away. 'Back in a tick. I'll just get the camera.'

Connor wanted to excuse himself as well but it would be kind of rude to walk out when Kate wasn't there. He felt uncomfortable enough being in here in the first place, without the unwanted attraction now simmering in his gut.

Good grief. Kate didn't even like being touched. Sex was out of the question. Wasn't it?

He had to get out of there. When Kate came back in, carrying a digital camera, Connor opened his mouth to give her the message he'd come with so he could leave, but the intention was interrupted by his pager sounding. He glanced at the screen.

'Can I make a call in here?'

* * *

'There's a phone right there.'

Kate was busy adjusting settings on the camera. She glanced up to tilt her head and indicate the location of the wall phone. Connor was wearing his leather jacket and looked as though he'd popped in here on his way home.

Why?

Because he wanted to see her at work? To see *her*?

They'd almost run out of reasons to spend time together under the umbrella of the joint project for Theatre and Kate had suspected that they would start spending less time together, so this was unexpected.

Nice.

She focused the camera on the evidence of the massive heart attack that had killed her patient. The sooner she finished this job, the sooner she could leave the hospital and maybe... Connor was going to ask her out somewhere.

Kate pushed the shutter button and then changed angles and pushed it again. She could hear Connor's voice and, after a surprised-sounding introduction to his conversation, his tone became oddly intense.

'Who is she...? How old...?'

He was being given quite a lot of information judging by the length of his listening time.

'What's the time frame? Okay... remind me what's involved on my part?'

He listened again. 'Might go for a local anaesthetic,' he said. 'Less down time. So, Monday, then? Seven-thirty a.m.? Got it.'

He hung up the phone but stood there staring at it for what seemed a long time.

'Problem?' Kate asked.

'Not for me.' Connor's voice sounded curiously thick. He cleared his throat. 'She's not even my patient.'

'Oh?'

'Little girl up in the ward. Lucy. She's seven and she's got leukaemia.'

Kate had finished her photography. She should dictate all her findings about the coronary arteries so she could complete her paperwork accurately later, but something wasn't making sense here. Something Connor had asked about what was involved on his part.

'Do you know her?'

'I've seen her. Totally bald from her chemo but she's got the biggest smile you've ever seen. Gorgeous kid.'

Something tightened in Kate's belly. An unpleasant sort of tightness which wasn't the sort she was used to associating with thoughts about Connor. This wasn't the first evidence that he liked children, was it? How had she managed to push that so far to the back of her head?

She stared at Connor and something must have shown on her face because he looked away.

'She needs a bone-marrow transplant,' he said. 'The family all lined up but they found a better match on the register. Me.'

Kate's jaw dropped. 'You're on a register to donate bone marrow?'

'Yeah... Been on it for a long time.'

'Have you ever made a donation?'

'Nope. This'll be the first.'

'So you're going to do it?'

'Sure.' Connor sounded surprised. 'Wouldn't you?'

'It wouldn't even occur to me to get tested in the first place to go on a register.'

'Don't you donate blood?'

'Of course I do. But that's nothing. They don't have to drill holes in my pelvis to get it out.'

Connor shrugged. 'Be a bit sore for a day or two, I guess. I don't mind.' He met Kate's stare. 'It's not a big deal.'

Was he kidding? It was a huge deal. Even for a close family member it would be a big deal to go through a bone-marrow donation, but Connor only knew this child by sight. By her smile.

The depth of care he gave his own patients was something that had blown her away, but this showed an even greater compassion. Was this kind of involvement instinctive for him because of how much he loved children?

What would he be like if he had children of his own?

He'd be an amazing father, that's what.

Maybe he couldn't wait for that to happen and that was why he got so involved with the children of total strangers.

The tight feeling inside Kate became sharper. Like a knife that was twisting and turning. Her voice came out much more sharply than she'd intended, as though that knife was real and not emotional.

'I can't believe how involved you get with your patients. With other people's patients, even.'

Connor seemed to grow taller. He was frowning. 'What are talking about?'

'I'm talking about the things you do for kids. Like riding a motorbike into a ward, for God's sake.'

'I didn't *ride* it. I wheeled it. And that was a one-off. It was—'

'You took me miles out of the city to sit on a hill above a beach to watch people surfing so I could understand how important Estelle's leg was for her.'

Connor's face was settling into an expression that managed to look both neutral and dangerous. 'You have a problem with that?'

'I think it's unhealthy to get too involved.' Kate wished she hadn't started this conversation but she couldn't turn back now.

Besides, she still had that nasty, sharp feeling in her belly.

'If you want to get that involved with kids,' she heard herself saying, 'you should get some of your own.'

That shocked him. He was staring at Kate as though she came from an alien species while she couldn't banish a series of images flashing through her head.

Connor holding a newborn baby. His own.

Passing it into the arms of the woman who had given him this gift.

A woman that wasn't Kate.

Oh, God... She wasn't going to cry. No way. Kate turned back to her dissection board.

'And if it's kids you want,' she added crisply, 'you shouldn't be wasting your time in here. With me.'

The silence from behind her was unnerving. She had to turn back.

'You don't really know me at all, do you?' Connor said.

Didn't she? Kate had thought she did. She'd danced with this man. She'd gone off with him willingly to do the most dangerous thing she'd ever done in her life, riding on the back of his bike. She'd dreamed about him. Okay, he might have no idea that he'd been sharing her bed so often, but it felt like she knew him very, very well.

Too well. Well enough to know that she could never get that close to him in reality.

But she couldn't say any of that aloud. After waiting for a long, long moment, Connor made a huff of sound that was both angry and defeated.

'Kids are the last thing I'd *ever* want,' he said bitterly.

* * *

He could hear the bitterness in his own voice.

See the absolute shock on Kate's face. Whatever else she had to get done before she could put the poor chap on the table back together had clearly been forgotten.

She was as shocked by his vehement statement as he had been when he'd discovered that someone had abused Kate in the past.

She'd been honest with him that night.

Didn't she deserve the same kind of honesty from him?

'Sorry,' he muttered. 'You touched a bit of a nerve.'

Kate nodded but her eyes were still bewildered. Connor blew out his cheeks in a long, long sigh.

'I'm the youngest of four brothers by quite a few years,' he told her. 'And the first real memory I have is from when I was about three and they brought our baby sister home from the hospital. Her name was Philippa but she was only ever called Pippi. Cos she was little and precious, my mother always said. The little girl she'd always dreamed of having.'

Kate looked as though she was holding her breath. As though she had no idea what to make of what he was telling her. Would she guess that he never talked about this? To *anyone*?

'Pippi got sick,' Connor continued. 'When she was almost four. Leukaemia was the first really big word I learned to say.'

He could see the sympathy in Kate's eyes so he turned his head just enough to focus on something else. It was way too late for sympathy.

'Things went okay for a few years,' he said. 'There were long hospital stays and chemo and a bone-marrow transplant. Everybody was completely determined that Pippi would get through it. Nothing else mattered. No one else mattered.'

Oh, God. Could Kate hear the self-pity that came through in the rough edge to his voice? How selfish was it, even after all these years, to feel that he'd been abandoned unfairly?

'Things went downhill when Pippi was six,' Connor went on relentlessly. 'I was lined up along with everybody else in the hope of finding a better match for a bone-marrow transplant. That was when my details got recorded, I guess, though they didn't contact me until I was over eighteen about going on the register.'

Turning his head again, Connor suddenly remembered

they were sharing this room with a dead person. He really did have to get out of here.

He faced Kate. 'Pippi died about six months after that and it broke what was left of my family. I wasn't quite ten years old when it happened. By the time I was fifteen I knew that I'd never want to have my own kids. They're a potential bomb waiting to go off and destroy a whole family. It's not a risk I'm ever going to take.'

Connor shook off the memories he'd never intended airing. 'A risk I *am* prepared to take is giving away some of my bone marrow in the hope that the same agony doesn't destroy the lives of others. If you think that's unhealthy or unprofessional, that's your problem, not mine.' The silence was unbearable.

Connor turned to leave. 'Oh... what I actually came down for was to tell you that the new microscope's arrived. I told them to leave things in the boxes because I thought you might want to supervise the unpacking tomorrow.'

He didn't give Kate a chance to respond.

'See you later,' was all he said. And then he walked out.

* * *

Very few people got put back together after an autopsy as neatly as Kate's latest research trial case.

She was working on autopilot and taking her time because she had too much else to think about.

Too many feelings welling up and swirling into a confused mess. It was comforting to let her hands do something as practical as suturing and cleaning instruments and tidying up.

Connor hadn't wanted her sympathy, that was for sure. He hadn't even given her a chance to say anything at all. She'd caught a glimpse of his face as he'd gone past on the other side of the glass window and the sadness on it had broken her heart.

Or it would have, if her heart hadn't already been broken by his story.

She could so easily imagine him as that little boy who knew his mother had only ever wanted a daughter. And no one else had mattered after Pippi got sick? That was easy to imagine, too. A household revolving around the hospital visits or taking care of a precious, sick child at home.

How much older than Connor were his brothers? Enough for them to have been a pack of their own? Maybe a pack that had stayed intact after the rest of the family got broken.

What about the forgotten child?

Kate's heart wasn't just broken. It was bleeding. Connor had felt unloved, hadn't he? She knew what that was like. Oh, God, she knew.

Kate wanted to reach back through the years. To pull that small boy into her arms and tell him that *he* was special too.

Loved.

He was loved now, she realised. Because all she wanted to do was find him. And hold him. And tell him that she understood.

That he was the most amazing, special person she'd ever met in her life.

No wonder he went far more than the extra mile for all his small patients and their families. For others that he barely knew apart from something like being bald and having a beautiful smile.

Kate could understand his determination not to have children of his own. Or for avoiding the risk of an intimate, long-term relationship. To give so much and make yourself so vulnerable only to have that love not returned or to get ripped out of your life. Heavens, he almost had a better reason than she did for being so determined. Something else they had in common that very few other people would.

It made them perfect for each other.

Didn't it?

Maybe... Kate finally turned out the lights and clicked the door of the morgue closed behind her.

If she could just...

She barely heard the farewell from the lone technician in the lab. Kate kept walking, her head down. Then she found herself straightening her back and looking ahead. Her stride lengthened.

Maybe she *could.*

But how was she going to make it happen?

* * *

Bella had checked twice that the oven was on.

Not that it was really necessary because she could smell the meat cooking. Kate was going to be so impressed with this. A rack of lamb and little baby potatoes. She'd even remembered to buy some mint sauce.

When the phone rang, Bella wiped her hands on her jeans and went to answer it.

'Is that Kate Graham's house?' a male voice asked.

'Yup.' It wasn't Connor, Bella realised. Shame. 'But she's not home at the moment. Can I take a message?'

There was a short silence. 'Maybe you could tell her... that her father called.'

Bella gave an audible gasp. 'You're Kate's *father*?'

'Yeah. I'm Kevin. Kevin Graham.'

'I'm Bella. Annabelle Graham. David's daughter. And...' Bella had to take a deep breath. 'And you're my grandfather.'

'Yeah.' There was a chuckle on the other end of the line. 'Surprise, huh?'

'Um...' Suddenly Bella didn't know what to say.

'I've been away,' Kevin said.

That was a euphemism and a half. But maybe he was ashamed of the fact he'd been in prison. Bella had the sudden urge to end the call. Kate wouldn't be happy about this, she could be absolutely sure of that.

What she'd never been sure of was why. This man, no matter what he'd done, was still a part of her family, wasn't he? Didn't people deserve a second chance?

'I just wanted to tell Kate I'm sorry,' Kevin said. 'I don't know what you got told, kid, but it was all my fault. Because of the drink, you know? And I'm clean now. Been off the stuff for years. It's part of the programme, to tell the people you've hurt that you're sorry.'

Bella had heard of that. She found herself nodding.

But what, exactly, had been all his fault? And would it make a difference if Kate knew how sorry her father was?

Maybe it would. What if the things that had happened so long ago were still affecting Kate now? If they were part of whatever it was that was keeping her and Connor from being more than just friends?

'She won't want to talk to me,' Kevin told Bella. 'But maybe she'll listen if you told her. I really mean it. It would mean a lot to be able to see her again and tell her for myself.'

If Kate could get past whatever it was, she might be able to move on with her life. It could be that Bella was being handed the opportunity to do something very important.

'Have you got a phone number?' she asked her grandfather. 'I need to think about this but I'll see what I can do.'

8

Kate knew exactly what she was going to do.

And she was going to do it on the weekend that Bella was going home to visit her parents and younger brother and sisters.

'I wish you'd come, too,' Bella said the night before she was due to leave. 'There's probably still time to grab a ticket.'

'I've got other things I want to do.'

'Like what?'

There was no way in the world Kate was going to let Bella in on her plans, never mind how much her niece would approve of them. Fate was on her side in looking for a distraction.

'What on earth is that?'

'What?' Bella was looking far too innocent.

'That noise. That...' Cocking her head to one side, Kate listened to get an idea of what direction the odd sound was coming from. Having identified that it was coming from Bella's room, Kate sighed and went hunting.

The scrap of a kitten was apparently not happy about being behind the closed door. It was a smoky grey colour with white on its paws and in patches on its face. A tiny pink mouth was open and the warbling, mewing sound was pathetic but definitely outraged.

'*Bella*! You know how I feel about pets. What on earth possessed you to drag a kitten home?'

Bella reached down and scooped up the tiny animal. 'But I didn't—'

'You'll have to take it back to the pet shop. What's the time? When do they shut?'

'I didn't get if from a pet shop. It was sitting on the doorstep when I got home.'

'Then ring the SPCA.'

Kate could hear the astonishingly loud purr the kitten was producing now. It climbed onto Bella's shoulder and rubbed its head along the line of her jaw.

'They must have a drop-off place,' she continued. 'For heaven's sake, you're going away in the morning. What were you planning to do? Just keep it shut in your room and hope I didn't notice? How irresponsible can you be, Bella?'

'I was going to tell you about it.' Bella was scowling. 'When you'd had a glass of wine or something so you were in a better mood.'

'There's nothing wrong with my mood. And a glass of wine isn't going to change my mind. I work all day. It's unfair to even think about having a pet.'

'Cats don't mind. They're not like dogs.'

'I don't like cats.'

'You liked Fluffy.'

'Fluffy was different. He was part of the family.'

'Well, this one could be part of a family, too. Your family.'

'I don't want a family.' Kate was not going to have the responsibility of something as huge as a pet to care for foisted on her like this. It was out of the question. Bella was not going to win this argument no matter how much she was scowling.

It wasn't until the words had rushed out of her mouth that Kate heard what she was saying and it stopped her in her verbal tracks.

Did she *really* not want a family?

'So you don't want me, then?' Bella sounded shocked. And then her eyes filled with tears.

'I didn't say that. That's not what I meant and you know it.'

Bella's head was bowed now. She was nuzzling the kitten, who put out a tiny, bright pink tongue and began enthusiastically washing Bella's chin.

'I just don't want a... a fur child,' Kate said desperately.

Why was the prospect so appalling? She'd loved Fluffy, the huge ginger cat that tolerated her brother's family. Was it because a pet of her own really would feel like a 'fur child'? Too close to the real thing?

'She chose us. *You.*' Bella's voice was muffled. 'She's an orphan and she chose your house. It's where she wants to live.'

'Someone's probably lost her and wants her back.'

Bella raised her gaze. 'So we could keep her until we find out who that is.'

'I... ah...'

'If she goes to the SPCA, she'll get locked in a cage. And there'll be older cats who might be mean to her. And they'll turn all the lights out at night and leave her all alone and she'll get cold and—'

'Oh, stop it.' A snort of laughter escaped Kate. 'All right. I suppose she can stay here until we find the owners. You can sort out the food and whatever toilet arrangements small cats need.'

She turned away with a sigh. 'It's just as well I'm not going away with you for the weekend, isn't it?'

'Mmm.' Bella gave her aunt a brilliant smile. 'You'll fall in love with her, you'll see. She'll fill the gap in your life.'

'I don't have a gap in my life.'

Bella's voice softened. 'Yes, you do, Kate. You just don't see it.'

It was Kate's turn to scowl. Any minute now and this was going to turn into an argument. Except that Bella was showering kisses on the kitten. And then she held it out towards Kate.

'This is the boss,' Bella informed the kitten. 'You'll have to behave yourself and earn your cat bikkies by keeping her company when I'm not here. We don't want Auntie Katie getting lonely at night, do we?'

* * *

It wasn't the company of a kitten to keep her from getting lonely at night that Kate had in mind, but she had to admit the distraction of the unexpected arrival had been welcome to keep nerves at bay.

Bella had found a pet shop open late on a Friday and they'd taken Kate's car and brought it home loaded up with pet food and bowls and a basket. Kate found the almost enclosed cat box that guaranteed to keep the house hygienic and added a stock of organic kitty litter to go with it. Bella found toys. A stick that had a string with feathers attached to the end. A tunnel that opened like a concertina. A scratchy post and a small laser light pointer.

'Ridiculous,' Kate muttered when they got home. 'All this stuff for just a few days.'

Bella, wise for once, said nothing.

On Saturday morning Kate had taken her to the airport and

then gone home via some specialist food and wine shops. She had a busy day planned. The house needed cleaning, including changing her bed linen. The dinner she was going to make would showcase some of her culinary skills. She had even planned to set aside some time to choose the perfect music to put on.

Kate was doing something she hadn't done in a very long time. She was hosting a dinner party.

And only one guest had been invited.

The kitten was a nuisance. It leapt onto the bed and got caught up in the sheets Kate was pulling off to put in the washing machine. She untangled it and put it on the floor. A corner from the armload of linen she carried out of the room was dangling and the kitten made a leap and swung from the sheet like an oversized pendulum.

'Oh, for heaven's sake!' But Kate found herself smiling. And if she hadn't had to deal with the kitten's determination to get involved in the task, she might have been left wondering what on earth she thought she was doing when it was highly debatable whether Connor would even get the chance to find out whether she had clean sheets on her bed. He hadn't responded to her casual invitation via text that she'd sent the moment she'd walked out of the airport terminal that morning. And why would he? The last time Kate had seen him had been when he'd walked out of the morgue, having revealed so much of himself. Had he regretted being so open? She hadn't seen him at all yesterday so maybe he was avoiding her.

The need to be close to him had preoccupied her all day after an almost sleepless night. She had gone over and over the things he had said and the implications his words had contained. And the more she thought about him, the surer she was of how much in love she was with Connor. And the more sure she was becoming that there could be a future for them.

It was a glorious day, this Saturday. Kate threw open the French doors to her living area in the heat of the afternoon and swept the courtyard. The kitten chased her broom.

'You're quite free,' she informed it. 'You're welcome to go back home if you want. I can always donate your accessories to a worthy cause.'

The kitten rubbed its head on her ankle. Kate went to make sure the barbecue's gas bottle wasn't empty. The fillet steak was already marinating in a mix of spices, including garlic and ginger. The potatoes were peeled, ready to cook and then crush and roast so that they would be hot and crispy and delicious. The food was going to be deceptively simple and hopefully irresistible to a large, hungry man.

Because Connor had finally responded to her text message with one of his own.

> You bet. I've been waiting for a chance to taste your food ever since Bella said you were the best cook in the world.

No pressure, then.

On her cooking or any other skills.

Kate had a quiet glass of champagne at 7 p.m., just before Connor was due to arrive.

The nerves were kicking in now. Kate was planning on testing a skill when she had no idea whether she even possessed it.

She had never even considered the notion of seducing a man before.

* * *

The setting was perfect.

Dusk had fallen and there were fat candles on the wooden table outside, the flicker of the flames reflecting on the crystal glasses and shining silverware. The barbecue was open and there were covered platters of things that were obviously about to get cooked, but even now he could smell something delicious.

The trees surrounding the small courtyard and garden closed them off from the world and Connor realised that he was feeling oddly nervous.

Had been, ever since Kate had opened her front door.

It had been the first time he'd seen her hair loose since that day he'd brought Bella home with her injured foot. A long time ago now and so much had changed. He knew so much about Kate.

She knew so much about him.

Maybe they both knew more about each other than anybody else on earth did. The thought was scary.

Not only was Kate's hair falling loose, she was also wearing a floaty sort of skirt that swirled around her legs when she moved. Connor had only ever seen her wearing fitted skirts at work or jeans at home. He'd never realised before how much more feminine it was to see the hints of leg that came and went between folds of soft fabric. So much... sexier. Her feet were covered in what looked like ballet shoes, but he could bet that underneath the pale leather, her toenails were bright red.

Good grief. He had to get a grip or he'd do something impulsive. Like reach for that silky, shining river of hair that was just begging to be stroked. Actually, what Connor really felt like doing was catching some of it and winding it around his hands until he'd trapped Kate's head so that he could position it perfectly to kiss her. Long.

And hard.

He swallowed hard and looked around. 'No Bella?'

'No.' Kate was fussing with the top of a wine bottle. 'She's gone home for the weekend to visit her family.' She cleared her throat. 'Would you like some wine or would you prefer a beer?'

'Wine's good. Here, give it to me.' He reached for the bottle, but Kate stepped away slightly.

'I can manage.'

Whoa... Connor slapped himself mentally. He should know how touchy Kate was about being given orders. Especially when it came to something she was perfectly capable of doing for herself. It wouldn't occur to her to feed a man's ego by pretending otherwise, would it?

And he liked that. Didn't he? She was a strong, independent woman who was at least his equal in pretty much everything. Except... she still needed protecting, didn't she? She was afraid of violence. Of letting people close.

Everything about this woman was confusing. Most confusing was the way he felt about her. Connor wasn't quite sure why he'd accepted the invitation to come to dinner tonight but now that he was here, one thing was very clear.

He wanted Kate.

And... maybe she wanted him, too. Otherwise why would she have set this up? She must have known Bella wouldn't be here and she'd obviously gone to a lot of effort to make things nice.

Nerves kicked in again. And when Connor felt something sharp attack his leg, he almost leapt out of his skin. He uttered a choice word he would never normally have chosen to say in front of a woman.

But Kate laughed. 'Meet the kitten,' she said.

The blasted animal was climbing purposefully up his jeans,

the heavy denim no match for claws that felt like needles. Connor carefully peeled the tiny animal away from his leg. It was no bigger than his hand. He looked at the ball of grey fluff. And then he looked up at Kate.

'Never would have picked you for a cat person,' he said.

'I'm not. Bella found it on the doorstep yesterday. I'm waiting for its owners to come and find it.'

'Seems happy.' He could feel the whole kitten vibrating with the rumble of its purr. 'I think it might prefer to stay here.'

'That's what Bella thinks.' Kate sighed. She handed Connor a glass of wine. 'But I've never even considered having a pet.'

'Why not?'

'Oh... you know. The whole "fur child" thing, I guess.' Kate met his gaze steadily. 'I'm probably further along the "no kids" road than you are. It extends to pets as well.'

The calm surety of her words was almost disturbing. In Connor's experience, all women wanted kids. They were happy with a relationship to start with but as soon as things started to get serious, he knew they were seeing wedding bells and babies. That was why those relationships never, ever lasted.

He'd known Kate was not his type. He'd known she was different. What he hadn't known was that her difference put her on the same planet he inhabited. They were two of a kind.

Made for each other?

Connor felt an odd sensation in his gut. It wasn't desire this time. It was a strange feeling. Like a smile that wasn't going to make it as far as his face. A sort of contentment.

It was a nebulous sensation, though. Newborn and fragile. Did Kate sense that he was at a bit of a loss? She picked something up from the table.

'Look at this.'

The device looked like a remote control for a car lock, but

when Kate pressed the button, the kitten scrambled from Connor's hands and shot across the flagstones of the courtyard like a bolt of furry lightning.

'What the—?'

And then Connor saw the red dot of the laser light that the kitten was chasing.

Kate was laughing again. She held out the device. 'Here, have a go while I get dinner started.'

Suddenly the tension had gone. Onto his second glass of wine with the entertainment the kitten was effortlessly providing, Connor realised he was thoroughly enjoying himself. He picked the kitten up and tucked it into the crook of his arm, rubbing it gently under its small white chin.

'You should keep it,' he told Kate. 'I've heard that the best cats are the ones that choose you, not the other way around.'

'Maybe I will. Shall I put the steaks on now or do you want to wait a bit?'

Connor didn't want the evening to end too soon. 'Let's wait.' He looked around. 'This is nice,' he pronounced. 'So peaceful.'

He smiled at Kate.

She smiled back.

And the silence suddenly seemed loud. Kate must have heard it too because he saw the way her eyes widened. Connor realised then that Kate was just as nervous as he'd been such a short time ago.

'Music,' she said hurriedly. 'I forgot to put it on. Darn.'

'Better late than never.'

It was like Kate had taken his nervousness and kept it. Connor felt confident now. Quite sure he was in the right place at the right time.

Kate was heading into the living area of her house. 'What do you like to listen to?'

'What have you got?'

'A bit of everything really. Except for country and western.'

'Thank goodness for that.' Connor followed her to the vintage-style turntable on top of a rack of vinyl records. He looked at the cover of the album she chose and tilted his head in agreement. He knew the music was slow. Romantic.

That smile feeling inside grew stronger. When the first lilting ballad filled the air and they had stepped outside again, Connor held out his hand.

'Shall we?'

Again, Kate's eyes widened but this time Connor saw them darken as well, and he knew that she wanted this as much as he did. She came into his arms willingly and, despite the unevenness of the courtyard surface, he found she was as easy to dance with as she'd been the night of that fancy-dress ball.

Not that they were doing anything particularly fancy. Slow dancing. Holding her close. His head bent lower over hers until he could touch his lips to the side of her neck.

And then Kate's head turned and her lips were right there. Soft and inviting.

He hadn't kissed Kate since that evening on the beach when she'd made it clear that she wasn't in the market for a relationship.

So much had changed between them since then. Had that conviction changed as well?

She certainly seemed to want this. Connor deepened the kiss and found Kate's tongue with his and the world began to spin away.

Until Kate surfaced to drag in a breath. 'Um... dinner?' she whispered.

'Forget dinner,' Connor growled. 'Where's your bedroom?'

* * *

She could do this.

She'd never wanted anything as much as this. Kate lifted her arms to help Connor remove her top. Her hair whispered against her bare skin and Connor's hands were tangled in its length.

'Your hair is amazing,' he said. He was holding chunks of it in his hands. Kate could feel her head anchored by the touch, but she didn't mind. Not when Connor's lips were on hers again. When his tongue was dancing with hers and it was making her feel that she wanted more. So much more.

She wanted it all.

And then her hair was released and Kate felt the strap of her bra being undone and Connor's hands came under her arms and touched her breasts, his thumbs grazing her nipples, and it felt exactly like it did in those dreams.

Only better.

Connor had shed his own shirt now.

His chest was broad, the muscles deliciously defined, with just a smattering of dark hair that arrowed down to the waistband of his jeans where he was undoing the fastening. He kept his eyes locked on Kate's and she couldn't look away.

Oh... Lord...

Kate's mouth went dry with desire while other parts of her body did quite the opposite.

And then he was naked. Huge and warm and intent on her. So intent, he stopped watching her face as he took off the rest of her clothes. They were skin-to-skin now and she could hear the rasp of Connor's ragged breathing as he pulled her so close she could feel the entire length of his body. It was like a dance move, the way he eased her onto the bed, and then he raised himself on one elbow, tracing her body with his other hand.

Her collar bone and her breast. The dip into her waist, his fingers trailing across her belly as his hand lowered. And then he touched her between her legs and Kate felt the first brush of panic.

No... This was Connor. She could do this.

But even as the battle waged behind her closed lids, Kate knew she was losing. She could feel herself pulling away. Back to the safe place where she could just watch what was happening to her body.

She couldn't feel it any longer. The thrill of Connor's touch was gone. It was pure mechanics and when the time came she would have to fake an orgasm. Just like she always had.

'Katie?'

Her eyes flew open. Connor had stopped touching her. He was looking at her instead and his face was very alert. The blurred intensity of unfulfilled desire had gone.

'What's wrong?' he asked quietly.

'Nothing.' Kate reached for him. 'Don't stop...'

But Connor caught her hands and held them. 'Talk to me,' he said. 'Tell me why you switched off like that.'

Kate was horrified. Admittedly the sample wasn't very large but to her knowledge, none of the men she had slept with had ever guessed where her head was. But why would they? She'd never started with them in the place she had started with Connor.

Wanting this so much.

Wanting *him*.

'I... don't know what you mean.'

Connor was silent. And Kate felt ashamed of herself for lying to him.

'I'm sorry,' she whispered.

Suddenly aware that she was lying there totally naked and exposed was horrible. Kate sat up, pulling her knees up so that she could wrap her arms around them. Connor seemed to simply melt out of the way, but Kate wasn't watching anyway. She buried her face against her bare knees.

'I thought I could do this,' she said. 'I thought it would work. I'm sorry, Connor.'

'I don't understand.' His hand touched her back and Kate couldn't help herself. She flinched.

The hand was withdrawn instantly and she heard Connor take in a slow breath. And then another one.

'That boyfriend of yours,' he said. 'He didn't just hit you, did he?'

Kate felt her breath escape in a kind of sob. 'No.'

'He raped you.' Connor's voice was as harsh as the word. 'My God, Kate. How old were you?'

'Fifteen. I... I wouldn't have sex with him. I was too scared. And when he hit me I was even more frightened and I tried to run away and... and...'

And Kate wanted to cry but the tears that might have been a relief were locked away along with all the wonderful feelings that Connor's touch had been able to give her.

Connor groaned. A desperately sad sound that only made Kate want to cry even more. 'It was too soon, that's all. You weren't ready for this.'

Kate shook her head. 'It won't work.'

'Don't say that.'

Kate felt the bed move as Connor stood up. She watched him through the tangle of her lashes as he stood beside the bed for a long moment and then he surprised her by turning and dropping to his knees.

'Kate, I don't know what's going on between us but it feels important. Important enough to be bigger than sex. We'll sort this out. You wanted me to make love to you, didn't you?'

'Yes.'

'And it was good until...'

Until he'd touched her so intimately? Kate nodded.

'So it can be good again.'

'You don't understand.' Kate's voice was weary. 'The only way I've ever been able to have sex with anyone was to distance myself. Kind of like the way you do when you have to do an autopsy or something. I didn't want to feel like that with you because...'

'Because what, Katie?' Connor's voice was gentle.

'Because I... care about you.' This was bad enough, without revealing just how much she cared about him. That was a grief that would have to stay very private. 'I thought it could be... I don't know... *real*.'

Connor's face looked grim now. He didn't know what to say. Or maybe he simply wanted to escape. Kate had to look away. Still, Connor didn't move. Did he need more of a reason? She could give him one.

'It's not just the sex that got screwed up for me,' she said quietly. 'There was a... a baby.'

She heard the sharp intake of his shocked breath.

'Oh, my God,' Connor breathed. 'Did it...? Did you...?'

'I lost it.' Kate clamped her lips together hard. That was all she was prepared to say. All she could say right now, without tearing the rest of her heart out, and if she did that, how could she survive?

'I'm sorry,' she said, yet again. She made her tone final this time. She rolled away to the other side of the bed. 'I'm going to the bathroom,' she told him. 'Maybe you should get dressed and go. You don't have to stay. I know how awkward this is... for both of us.'

'You don't want me to stay?' The query was almost expressionless. More of a statement than a question.

'Best you don't.'

Kate tried to swallow the lump in her throat but it wouldn't go away. This failure on her part was so huge it was mortifying. Talking about it any more wouldn't help. Being naked with him was unbearable now, even though she was standing with her back to Connor and knew that her hair was enough of a shield. She had tried. And failed. There was no going back from that. And there was no going forward either.

'This isn't going to work, Connor,' she said. 'Let's just forget it.'

Rustling sounds from behind her suggested that Connor was collecting his clothing. Kate didn't wait to see him get dressed or show him out of her house. She went into her en suite bathroom and closed the door behind her.

* * *

The French doors were closed and locked now.

The barbecue turned off, the uneaten food packed away in the fridge. The music had been silenced and the candles had been snuffed out, but Kate didn't bother turning on any other lights.

She was sitting, curled up on one end of the couch, her back to an armrest and her knees drawn up so that she could hug them. Like the way she'd been sitting on the bed when she'd wanted to hide her nakedness.

She was fully clothed again now but she still felt naked. Exposed. Taken back to place she would never be able to escape from. The horror of being shouted at and ordered to do things that terrified her. The pain of that attack. The repercussions.

Locking it away had seemed to be the answer that had come to her with blinding inspiration that day she'd found the rusty old key in that junk shop. How could it have occurred to a broken teenager that it would all come back to haunt her? That it was an obstacle she would never get past no matter how badly she wanted to?

Well, she would just have to deal with it. Much safer to be alone and not risk the kind of pain that came from realising what she was missing out on.

What Connor could have given her.

What she could have given him.

Bella had hit the nail on the head when she'd said that Kate had a gap in her life. What she hadn't been right about was saying that Kate didn't know what it was. She knew exactly what it was.

That magic that was so much bigger than the simple addition of two parts. The power and strength that was created by a shared love between two people who chose to share their lives intimately. Kate was too miserable to notice that the kitten had climbed onto the couch and snuggled its way into the gap between her knees and her chest. She barely noticed the way she responded to the push of the little grey head by stroking it.

There was something comforting about the movement, though. Kate stroked the kitten from its head to where that ridiculous triangle of a miniature tail began. Again and again.

She could feel the softness of its fur. The tiny knobs of a spine. The rumble of the purr. The sensation filled her fingertips and travelled into her hands and up her arms. All the way to her heart, and Kate knew that Bella was right about something else, too.

She was falling in love with this kitten.

She could feel the pleasure of stroking it. Her nerve endings were hungry for it. And they weren't going to get switched off by a mechanism Kate couldn't control because she knew perfectly well that this touch was not threatening in any way.

And finally, the tears came. Years and years and years' worth of tears.

9

Nobody had come knocking on the door to claim the kitten.

Kate actually seemed keen to keep it now. She had given it a name. Bib, because that's what the white patch under her chin looked like.

Bella should have been delighted by this turn of events, and normally she would have been. Over the moon, in fact. But something was wrong.

She'd come back on Sunday night. Kate had cooked the most amazing dinner of deliciously marinated steaks and crispy, crushed potatoes, but she hadn't been hungry herself so why had she gone to so much effort?

It hadn't taken Bella very long at all to work out what it was that was bothering her so much. She had, in fact, recognised what it was before that dinner was even finished.

It was that glow. Kate just didn't have it any more and it seemed like the sun had stopped shining or something. When she asked whether Kate had had a good weekend, her aunt had answered with that kind of brightness that let you know you were being fobbed off. That something was very wrong but it wasn't any of your business.

Bella hated being shut out. Always had. And hadn't that refusal led to the close bond she had with Kate in the first place? She'd seen her go off, looking so miserable that day, and had gone after her, despite her parents telling her to leave Kate alone. That she wasn't happy and probably needed a bit of time to herself to get used to things. Following her instincts had turned out all right that time, hadn't it?

But Kate wasn't storming off anywhere this time. She was just being... Kate. Tidy and organised and working all hours. Maybe that was the problem. She'd seen Kate break out of that normality the day she'd gone off on the back of Connor's bike and she'd liked that. A lot.

Something had happened to change things.

Maybe it had something to do with Connor.

Or maybe it had something to do with her grandfather getting out on parole and trying to contact his children.

Bella had tried to talk to her father about it. She didn't tell him about the phone call, she just tried a tentative query about the family in general that had led to a question about her grandfather.

Don't even go there, her father had warned. *Especially in front of Kate.*

Even Bella hadn't had the nerve to ask why not but she was thinking it. Did they not know that her grandfather had got himself sober? That he was full of remorse for whatever it was he'd done? That he wanted to at least start putting things right by apologising?

No wonder Bella was feeling shut out.

And cross.

Even crosser today because work had not gone well.

'He's unbelievable,' she informed her aunt over dinner.

'Who is?'

'Mr Dawson. Oliver Dawson.'

'The neurosurgeon?'

'That's the one.' Bella's scowl deepened.

'What's wrong with him?'

'He shouted at me.'

'Oh?' Kate had stopped picking at her meal and looked at Bella. 'What did you do wrong?'

'Why do you assume that it was my fault?'

Kate actually smiled and Bella realised it was the first smile she'd seen for days. Oh, well. That was something, she supposed.

She rolled her eyes. 'It wasn't as if I was in there as a scrub nurse or anything. And the operation hadn't even started yet. There was no reason for me to have done my mask up properly. I was nowhere near the table.'

'What did Oliver say?'

'That his theatre wasn't some kind of nursery and if I needed to wear a bib I should go and find a day-care centre or something.'

Kate's lips twitched. The kitten must have learned its name already because it jumped into Bella's lap. Then it tried to climb onto the table. Bella lifted it clear before Kate could growl and she cuddled it under her chin.

'He's so stuffy,' she went on. 'Old and stuffy and… and…'

'And very good at his job by all accounts,' Kate said mildly. 'And he's younger than me, thanks very much. I don't think he's much over thirty, in fact.'

'Well, he acts like he's fifty.'

'He's conservative, certainly,' Kate agreed. 'But his upbringing probably has a lot to do with that.'

'What – was he brought up in a monastery or something?'

Kate chuckled. 'Not far off. Don't you know about the Dawson family?'

'No. Should I?'

'One of the wealthiest families in Auckland. Pillars of society and all that. Oliver was an only child and his social responsibilities were probably drummed in from an early age. I suspect he has very high standards in everything he does and that's why he's such a good surgeon. And why he expects everybody else to follow the rules.'

Bella snorted. 'I prefer people that break the rules occasionally. Like Connor.'

The sudden chill in the atmosphere was unmistakeable.

'Had enough?' Kate asked briskly. She stood up and whipped Bella's plate away before she had time to do more than start nodding her head. And then she stood with her back to the table, rinsing the plates to go into the dishwasher.

Bella stared at the plait hanging down Kate's back. It bounced occasionally, as if the body it belonged to was very tense and its movements were jerky.

So *that* was what it was all about.

It wasn't anything to do with her grandfather.

Or was it?

Bella stroked Bib thoughtfully, her mind going back over what was now a well-worn track. How could you move on into a peaceful future if there were things in the past you hadn't sorted out?

She thought about the scrap of paper she was using as a bookmark. It was in her room, marking the point she'd reached in her latest romance novel. A mobile phone number that she could text rather than ring, which would be good because it could be secret.

It would have to be somewhere neutral, she decided. She knew it would be totally the wrong thing to do to invite her grandfather to visit Kate's house. The frisson of something like fear that trickled down her spine at the very idea was a warning bell. Kate would never forgive her if that turned to custard.

But somewhere neutral. Public, even? Like a coffee shop?

No. Bella suddenly knew the answer. What was needed was a place where Kate could feel in control. That was the key. And there was only one place other than her home where Kate wielded real power.

The pathology department.

'Want some help?' she asked Kate casually.

'No. There's not much to do.'

'I might have an early night then. I've got a book I really want to finish.'

* * *

Work was the answer.

Normal life had resumed.

The clock had been wound right back to before Kate had noticed those tyre marks on the lino of the hospital corridor.

People had noticed how focused she was and her whole department seemed to be suddenly more professional. The pace was brisker. Okay, maybe she was a bit less tolerant and that was making her junior staff members wary, but they were working harder as well. Mark, in particular, was trying extremely hard to stay in favour.

And he was succeeding. So much so he deserved a reward.

'How would you like to be involved in the new theatre laboratory?'

'That would be great. I didn't know it was up and running yet.'

'It's not, quite. The new equipment's arrived, though. You could go and get things set up and I'll come and check later.'

'Don't you want to do it? It's your baby.'

'It's a departmental project,' Kate said dismissively. 'That's all.'

It was harder than she'd expected to get past this particular wrench of the clock being turned back. Estelle had been discharged from hospital now, well on the way to recovery, but that whole incident had been the start of getting close to Connor, hadn't it? And then the planning for the mini laboratory had kept the wheels turning long enough to go way too far down that track.

Well, it was over now. She hadn't even seen Connor for the last couple of days but Kate didn't want to risk an encounter too soon and she needed to stay away from Theatre. Which was a shame because she'd really looked forward to taking her turn in staffing that laboratory space. Being right there, literally at the cutting edge, of what a good part of her job was all about, instead of being shut away in the bowels of the hospital.

It took a great deal of courage to go up and check that Mark had set up the microscope and other equipment correctly, but Kate needn't have worried. Connor wasn't there. Bella was, however.

'What time are you finishing work?' she asked.

'No idea. I've got a bucket of stuff to get finished, including a write-up on that research trial I'm involved in. I might be late so don't wait for me.'

'Okay.' Bella seemed oddly pleased that Kate was planning to work late.

Kate took another glance around the busy corridor in the theatre suites.

'He's not here,' Bella said.

'Who?' Was she still bothered about her run-in with Oliver Dawson?

'Connor.'

'What on earth makes you think I was looking for him?' Kate gave her words a warning edge but Bella merely shrugged.

'Just in case you were. He's not here. He got sent home.'

He was sick? The clutch of concern took Kate by surprise, but she didn't say anything. She couldn't. The ferocity of that concern was disturbing enough to render her speechless for a moment.

'Apparently he did a bone-marrow donation yesterday morning. Can you believe that? For a little girl who's got leukaemia.'

Still Kate said nothing. Of course she could believe it. And why he would go to such extraordinary lengths to help a little girl and her family. That had been the final push to falling completely and utterly in love with him.

'He got it done under local and came back to work this morning, but he was still really sore so he got sent home to rest.'

'I... imagine it would be a fairly painful procedure.'

'Mmm...' Bella seemed to be watching her more closely than Kate felt comfortable with.

'I'll see you later, then,' she said, edging away.

Kate planned to keep herself as busy as possible for the rest of the day, inventing extra work if necessary, because that was the only way to stop herself thinking about Connor. Worrying about the possible complications that might come from having holes drilled in your pelvis. Worrying that he might be trying to be far too macho and avoiding taking any kind of pain relief.

As it turned out, Kate didn't have to find any extra work. It found her, in the form of a forensic examination of a suspicious death. Lewis Blackman was back on deck and claimed he was feeling better than ever, but Kate didn't want him overdoing things.

'I'll do it,' she told him. 'You can supervise.'

A forensic examination was far more detailed than an ordinary autopsy. Right from the start, when the body bag was opened, photographs had to be taken and every detail recorded to appear in the paperwork. This was quite clearly a homicide so the hands of the victim were encased in plastic bags. When they were opened, scrapings from under the fingernails had to be collected, labelled and stored. Every item of clothing had to be documented before being removed and it was only then that the medical examination could begin. Wounds could be examined and photographed and then, after the body was cleaned, they could start to look for the actual cause of death.

In this case, it was a matter of determining which, out of many, of the stab wounds had been the lethal blow and it was time-consuming because the angle and depth of each injury needed to be measured. The whole procedure took several hours and it would take at least another hour to do the paperwork involved. Lewis offered but Kate shooed him home.

'You look tired,' she said. 'And it's getting late. I was planning to do some office work for a while anyway.'

When Lewis left, the department was curiously empty. A technician had gone on blood-testing rounds and the others must have gone for a meal break. Not that Kate minded the solitude. It meant that she didn't need to shut the door of her office or close the venetian blinds on the windows that looked out into the lab. She did jump when she heard the rapid footsteps of someone approaching. She went out of her office to see who it was and then stopped in astonishment.

'Bella! What on earth are you doing here? I thought you would have gone home long ago.'

'Um... I came to see you.' Bella smiled brightly.

'I'm kind of busy.'

'Oh... well, I might have a look around, if that's okay. I've never been down here before. What's that machine for?'

'It measures the oxygen level in arterial blood.'

'Cool. And that one?'

'It's an X-ray for checking biopsy samples before we slice them up. Look, Bella, I really do have work to do.'

Bella glanced over her shoulder. She bit her lip. She looked at her watch. 'Fine. I'm going...'

Except she didn't. She loitered for another minute or two, staring around as if she was fascinated by everything she could see. And then there was the sound of another person approaching and when the figure filled the doorframe, Kate felt the blood drain from her head, leaving her feeling faintly dizzy and rather ill.

'Oh, Bella...' The words were a whisper. 'What *have* you done?'

* * *

Connor felt terrible.

It wasn't his hip that was bothering him. That felt a lot better. He'd been stood down from working today but he hadn't gone home like he probably should have. He'd gone and got a few hours of restless sleep in an on-call room. Then he'd given in and taken a painkiller and had had a few hours of much better quality sleep.

Now he needed a shave and something to eat but he knew it wouldn't make him feel good because it wasn't anything physical that he was having trouble dealing with.

It was the fact that he'd been such a coward.

Kate had given him an easy way out and he'd taken it.

Not immediately, of course. He'd stayed there in her bedroom that night, having got dressed again, and he'd paced about, staring at the statement being made by the closed door of that en suite bathroom.

He would stay, he decided. They couldn't leave things like this.

They needed to talk about it.

But where would he start?

How on earth could he hope to undo even part of so much damage? He'd been horrified enough that Kate had lived with an abusive father, but he'd been confident that he could handle that.

Fix her, even.

But this – the knowledge that she'd been *raped*... that she could only bear a man's intimate touch by distancing herself as though she was performing an autopsy?

That had been overwhelming. He didn't think he could have been any more shocked, but he had been when Kate had mentioned the baby.

Pregnant as the result of a rape? Unthinkable.

What had she done? Had the pregnancy terminated? Had the baby adopted? Had a miscarriage because her father had beaten her up when he'd found out about the pregnancy?

Did it actually matter?

No. What mattered was that it seemed to have been as damaging as the rape because Connor had known that, however it had been conceived, that baby had been loved.

I lost it, was all she'd said. And she'd lost so much more than that, hadn't she? She'd lost – or maybe she'd never discovered – the joy of sex. She'd lost a part of her family. She might have been broken in a different way from what he had been, but the result was eerily similar. An aversion to the kind of closeness that could bring pain in its wake. He was better off than she was, though, wasn't he? At least the release and pleasure of sex was something he'd enjoyed all his adult life.

Yeah... Kate's history was worse than his own. All the more disturbing because he could understand the space it had left her in. A walled-off space.

A barrier that was far more solid than the door of that bathroom.

Kate didn't want him to still be there when she came out and Connor could finally understand why Kate had such a need to be in control of what was around her. It was why her house was so perfect and why she kept people at such a distance.

If he was still there, he would be undermining that control and that would hardly be a good place to start, would it?

Besides, he'd needed to think.

And think he did. Long and hard. His head told him to back away.

But his heart wasn't going to let him do that.

Funny how you could see something when it was happening to somebody else and it was only then that you recognised it was happening to you.

Kate was crippled by the fear of emotional pain that came from loving someone and losing them. She couldn't even go through the motions of expressing love physically because she had distanced herself from love far more than he had. But she was missing out on the most important thing that life had to offer.

Not sex, though that was a part of it, certainly.

Kate was missing out on the joy of sharing her life. Of a loving relationship that brightened joy and dimmed sorrow. The strength that could come from being with someone who could understand. Who could give – and receive – love.

And so was he.

They could both get so much more out of life by taking that risk.

And maybe... just maybe... they could take it together.

He didn't get a chance to get near Kate on Monday morning because he'd had such an early start for that bone-marrow collection procedure, and he'd felt far worse afterwards than he'd expected so had had no choice other than to go home for the day.

He'd come back this morning only to be told how awful he looked and, if he was limping that badly, there was no way he'd stay on his feet long enough to be able to operate safely.

So he'd slept. He'd taken the painkillers and slept well enough for the healing process to get properly under way. He might still be limping a bit but he could move.

He was moving. It was late in the day but, if he was in luck or it was meant to be, maybe Kate was working late. More slowly than he would have liked, Connor made his way down to the pathology department.

* * *

The look on Kate's face would have frightened anybody.

This had been a bad idea, after all, but it was too late to do anything about it. Kevin Graham had followed her directions and turned up, after hours as instructed, to visit his daughter.

He was a much bigger man than Bella had anticipated and he looked nothing like she had expected. His clothes were scruffy and his face was hard, and he smelled like... like...

'You've been drinking,' Bella gasped. 'You told me you were doing the twelve steps. That you hadn't had anything to drink for years.'

'Hadn't.' Kevin walked further into the lab, his gait only mildly unsteady. He waved a paper bag he was holding in one hand, screwed up at the top so he didn't lose his grip on the bottle it contained. 'Just needed a bit of, you know, Dutch courage.'

He was smiling but it didn't do anything to make him a more appealing figure. 'Hello, Katherine. Long time no see. How's things?'

'Get out,' Kate snarled. 'Bella, get on the phone over there and call Security.'

'Don't do that.' Kevin's eyes narrowed as he walked closer. 'That wouldn't be very friendly, would it? Didn't the girl tell you that I just wanted to say I was sorry?'

Kate took a step back. '*Sorry*? What for? Murdering my mother?'

Bella's jaw dropped. 'Oh, my God... you're a *murderer*?' She turned to Kate. 'I didn't know. I'm sorry, Kate. I really didn't know...'

'No.' The word was clipped. 'But now you do.'

'I'm sorry. Alright?' Kevin raised his voice. 'I've done my time. You have to at least let me say that I'm sorry.'

'I don't have to do anything.' Kate's voice was cold. 'I don't want to hear you or see you ever again. Get out of here. Get out of my life.'

Kevin swore loudly and viciously. 'I might have known,' he said. 'I'm wasting my time, aren't I? You're not going to listen to a thing I say. You're just like your mother. Won't listen. Won't do as you're told.'

Kevin was moving again. Walking towards Kate, who was edging behind an island bench in the middle of the lab. She looked terrified.

Bella had had enough. She had caused this horrible situation and she was going to do something about it. She darted in front of Kevin.

'Get out,' she said. 'You can't stay here. You shouldn't have come.' Bella glared at the man. Her grandfather? No. It was unbelievable.

Kevin's hand shot out so fast Bella didn't see it coming. The slap was enough to knock her off her feet and make her ears ring. She pushed herself up. Kate was trying to reach the phone on the wall near the door. Kevin was clearly planning to prevent her. Bella stepped behind him but Kevin must have heard her coming because he turned and gave her a shove that sent her flying again.

'Get out, Bella,' Kate shouted. 'Get help. Now.'

* * *

Connor was halfway along a deserted corridor in the basement of St Pat's when he saw a figure hurtle through the department door and fall to the floor, uttering a cry of pure fear. Ignoring the stab of pain, Connor picked up speed until he was running.

He could see it was Bella, but that wasn't what made him run faster.

Instinct told him that it was Kate who was in trouble somehow.

He'd put his life on the line if that's what it would take to keep Kate safe.

He couldn't do anything else.

Because it was in that moment of time that he realised just how much he loved her.

10

'*Connor...*' Bella was sobbing. 'He's trying to kill her.'

Connor didn't even slow down as he reached the door. 'Who?'

'Her father.' Bella was fumbling for her phone, trying to flip it open.

There was the sound of glass smashing within the lab. Connor pushed the door open with a bang and then stopped to get his bearings and see what was going on.

Kate was behind an island bench. The intruder was on the other side, using his arm to sweep a microscope and racks of glass vials to the floor with a vicious jerk of his arm. Then he saw Connor. 'Who the hell are you? Get out. This is between me and my kid.'

'Deal with Kate and you deal with me,' Connor told him.

'*Ooh...*' The sound had an unpleasant, suggestive tone. 'Fancy her, do you? You'd better watch out. She's a bolshie little cow. Just like her mother was.'

Raising his arm, the man hit the side of the bench with something he was holding in his hand. A bottle. Connor could see the jagged edges of the weapon like knives protruding from shreds of brown paper. He waved it in front of him, jabbing towards Connor. And then his head turned towards Kate, and Connor knew what he was planning.

'Get down, Kate,' he yelled. 'Get on the floor.'

He couldn't stop to consider her aversion to being shouted at or ordered around. This was for her safety, for God's sake...

Except she wasn't moving. She was staring at Connor and he could see the desperation in her face. Without thinking, he launched himself into a rugby-style tackle that would have earned praise on a football field.

He wasn't tackling the angry, drunk man, however. Connor launched himself at Kate. He reached her and caught her body, taking her with him for the rest of the fall, just as the half-broken bottle was hurled at the space she'd been standing in. He felt the buttons pop off the white coat she was wearing and knew her glasses had gone flying.

He heard a howl of rage from the man and new missiles were being found and thrown. Connor kept his body on top of Kate's. Holding her still. Something hard hit him painfully on one shoulder and he tried to curve himself to cover more of Kate. She lay rigid beneath him. He would have to let her go so that he could get up and deal with their attacker, but not just yet. Not until there was a pause in this ferocious onslaught.

And then Connor heard new sounds. Shouting and banging. He raised his head to see two burly security men storming into the lab. Bella was peering round the edge of the door behind them, her face as white as a sheet. It took only moments for the security men to overpower the man.

'Who is this creep?' one of them asked. 'And how the hell did he get down here?'

'It was my fault.' Bella wasn't crying now. She looked

agonised as she crept into the lab. 'Kate? Where are you? Oh, God... are you alright?'

Connor eased himself off Kate but didn't take his weight completely off her body. He knelt over her, reaching for her face with his hands. Holding it so that she had to meet his searching gaze.

'You're safe,' he said softly. 'You know that, don't you?'

* * *

She felt safe.

How ridiculous was that? Her worst nightmare had just happened, having to confront her father again in one of his blind, drunken rages. He was still there, breathing the same air that she was. Connor had yelled at her. He'd thrown himself at her and it should have felt like a physical assault, and yet Kate felt completely safe.

Because it had been Connor who had grabbed her. Because he was here. Because he was looking at her like... like her safety was the only thing that mattered in the whole world.

And you could only look like that if you loved someone.

As much as she loved him?

Kate let Connor help her up. He found her glasses, fortunately unbroken, and handed them to her to put back on. She didn't want to lose the touch of his body so soon, though, so she stood close to Connor, pressed to his side, grateful for the arm that came around her and didn't move again.

'I'm fine,' she told Bella, although she wasn't sure how true that was. Her legs felt oddly shaky. Her hands were trembling. It had been quite a mission to settle her glasses into the right spot on the top of her nose.

'So who is this guy?' the security man asked again.

'I'm her *father*,' Kevin snarled.

'No.' Kate sucked in a jagged breath. 'You've never been a father to me. I knew that even before you murdered my mother.'

'*Whoa*...' The younger security guard looked shocked. 'This guy's a murderer? Good thing we've got the cops on the way.'

'You'll find he's probably on parole,' Kate told them. 'He was on parole once before, years ago, and got locked up again because he beat someone senseless in the first pub he went into.'

'Doubt he'll ever be getting out again, then,' the older guard said. He jerked Kevin in front of him to start him walking. 'We'll take him outside.' He looked back as he reached the door. 'The police will be wanting a statement from you guys. Don't go away yet, will you?'

He took another look at Kate. 'Will you be okay? Want us to send someone else down to stay with you?'

Kate pressed closer to Connor. 'I'll be okay.'

'She will be,' Connor growled. 'I intend to make sure of it.'

* * *

The pathology department was being sealed off with wide, bright red 'Crime Scene' tape stretched from one side of the doorframe to the other.

Bella watched with some dismay. She'd already been here far longer than she liked. She should never have come in the first place. She certainly shouldn't have suggested that Kevin Graham come here to make contact with his long-lost daughter. The sooner she could escape the better but, as far as she knew, that door to the main corridor was the only exit.

'Aren't we allowed to go home?' she asked.

'We don't want anything moved until the scene's been photographed,' a police officer explained. 'And some fingerprint evidence has been collected. That tape's to keep people out, not to keep you in, though it would be better if we all stayed in this office until they've finished. It shouldn't take long.'

'All' was two police officers, Bella, Connor and Kate. There were only two chairs in Kate's office. Kate was sitting in one and Bella in the other. Connor had a hip hitched onto the desk, and the leg touching the floor was also touching Kate's chair. Touching Kate, even? Bella tilted her head to try and see but, instead, she caught Kate's glance.

A new wave of misery made her cheeks flush and her eyes sting. This was all her fault and if it hadn't been for Connor happening to come along at the right moment, it could have been a tragedy.

'So your father was found guilty of manslaughter?' A police officer had been taking notes busily for a while now.

'The jury had no hesitation in convicting him,' Kate told them. 'Not that I attended the trial, but my brother did. A neighbour from across the road heard the argument and could actually see him pushing Mum across the room. She fell down the stairs, hit her head and died two days later without regaining consciousness.'

Kate's voice was remarkably steady, but Bella saw the way Connor reached down to squeeze her shoulder. 'David also gave evidence about the abuse we'd suffered as children.'

Bella hung her head. If only she'd known. She could understand now that kind of secret pact Kate and Bella's father had shared. And no wonder they hadn't wanted to talk about it. It was horrible to think that you were related to a monster like that. An addiction to the alcohol that fuelled the rages was no excuse at all.

'He got sentenced to fifteen years,' Kate was saying now. 'He managed to get parole after twelve by convincing the board that he was sober and he'd stay that way. He lasted two days, I believe, before he got into a fight at a pub and nearly killed someone else.'

'He'll never get out this time,' the police officer assured her. 'No judge is going to take a risk like that.'

'Good.' Kate looked up at Connor as though she could sense him watching her.

The eye contact held for a significant beat of time. Long enough to make Bella hold her breath for a moment. Was she missing something here? Were they...?

Kate's gaze swung to meet her own and Bella blushed.

'I'm so sorry.' She'd lost count of how many times she'd said it, but she'd keep saying it for as long as she needed to. And she would never, ever, meddle with anyone else's business again.

'I'm still confused about how he found out where Kate worked,' a police officer said.

'It was me,' Bella sighed. She told them all about the phone call she'd had from her grandfather that she'd kept secret from Kate and about her texted instructions for the meeting she'd set up.

'He really sounded sorry,' she said. 'And I believed him. And I know that Kate's always so fair and that if people deserve it, they will always get a second chance.'

They were looking at each other. *Again*. Kate and Connor. And this time there was more than a hint of a smile on both their faces. A private, significant sort of smile.

By the time the police had finished the interview, the photographer and fingerprint technician were also finished and they were told they were free to go home.

'We'll be in touch if we need anything more before the trial date gets set.'

Bella stood up to follow the police officers. When she turned to see if Kate was going to come home with her, she found Connor and Kate looking at each other. Again. And this time they were holding hands.

Bella had to clear her throat to get noticed.

'You go on,' Kate told her. 'I need a minute or two to get my head together and maybe tidy up a bit.'

Bella hesitated.

'Don't worry,' Connor said. 'I'll look after her.'

He would, too. Bella could see the way he was looking at Kate and for the first time since this whole horrible thing had happened, Bella could feel a bubble of something good inside. Something was going on between Kate and Connor that hadn't been there before.

Something really *good*.

She really did need to get out and give them some time alone, but still she hesitated.

'It's okay, Bells,' Kate said. 'I'm not mad at you. You honestly believe the best of people and most of the time it's a very good trait to have. And, you know, you might have just done us all a favour.'

'*What*?' The word came out as a surprised squeak.

'It sounds like they're going to lock Kevin up and throw the key away this time and that's going to keep us all safe. You brought things out into the open and that's probably where they should have been all along. Secrets can be destructive.'

She looked up at Connor and smiled, and Bella knew she was really, really in the way now.

'I'm going,' she announced. 'I'm going to ring Mum and Dad

and confess before they hear about it from anyone else. Especially the police. I'll see you later.'

The 'Crime Scene – Do Not Disturb' tape had been torn off one side of the doorframe. Bella paused and looked over her shoulder to see Connor closing the door of Kate's office. Then she saw his hands reach for the venetian-blind control, shutting the office into a completely private space.

Bella's lips twitched. This couldn't be counted as meddling, could it?

She picked up the end of the red tape and stuck it back on the doorframe. The cleaners and anybody else would just have to wait a while.

* * *

Kate watched Connor close and lock the door of her office and close the blinds, giving them privacy.

This was the furthest he'd been away from her since he'd barrelled into her with that rugby tackle that had probably saved her from getting half a broken bottle in her face.

The memory of how real the danger she'd been in had been seemed to be causing some kind of delayed reaction now that it was finally all over and everybody else had gone. Kate was trembling all over.

'Oh, Katie…' The tenderness in Connor's voice undid her completely. Kate took his outstretched hands and let him pull her to her feet and into his arms.

'Hold me,' she whispered. 'Please… I want to feel safe.'

'You are safe,' Connor whispered back. 'I'm here. I'm not going anywhere. I love you, Kate.'

Safe. Yes, despite the trembling, Kate did still feel safe. Safer than she'd ever felt in her life because, for the first time, she wasn't totally responsible for her own safety like she had been when she'd been keeping those dark secrets. Connor knew almost everything about her and... he loved her?

Kate had to pull back to look into his face and search for confirmation of those miraculous words.

And it was there. In the way he was looking at her. In the love she could see in his eyes. In the way his hands were holding her. Loosely now, so that his hands could stroke her body.

'I should never have let you send me away the other night, but I didn't know what to say. Or do. I'm so sorry, Kate.'

She shook her head. He had nothing to be sorry for.

'I didn't want you to think I was trying to take control,' he continued. 'To tell you what to do. I didn't know what to do. I needed to think. To figure things out.'

He sounded so sincere. So... confident?

'And did you? Figure things out?'

Connor nodded slowly. 'I reckon. I wasn't sure until I was standing outside the department and I saw Bella and I knew you were in danger, and then I knew.'

'Knew what?'

'How much I love you.'

Kate's vision misted. 'I love you, too, Connor. You're... amazing.'

A hint of a smile tugged at his lips. 'It's going to be all right, you know.'

'What is?'

'Us. Life. We both know what it's like not to be loved. We've both been too scared to take the risk of loving someone in case it happened again, but it's not going to happen again, Katie. Not ever. I can't *not* love you, do you understand? Not ever.'

'Oh...' Kate breathed. 'I understand.'

Of course she did. It was the way she felt about Connor. Her love for him was a part of every cell of her being. If it went away, she would cease to exist.

'We're perfect for each other,' Connor whispered. 'And that makes anything possible. Making love... Making a baby, even.'

The flutter of panic was muted but it was still there. Enough to make Kate's body tense involuntarily.

'You're going too fast,' she gasped.

'I'm sorry.' Connor pulled her close again and this time he was rocking her gently. The tension ebbed and a soft warmth stole through Kate.

'I want you,' Connor murmured just above her ear. 'I want everything. I want to marry you, Katie.' She felt his chest heave as he took a very deep breath. 'That's all I really need. Could you go that far?'

Kate had to swallow past the constriction in her throat. 'Yes...' she managed. 'Oh... *yes*.'

The distance between them increased as though they both needed to see the face of the other. For a long, long moment they stared at each other, soaking in the wonder of the words that had just been spoken. The promise that had been made.

The hope that the future suddenly held.

Connor's face wasn't quite clear, however. Were tears blurring her eyes? Kate reached under her glasses to wipe them away and felt them being lifted from her face.

'You don't need those right now,' Connor told her. He put them down on the desk behind them and then turned back with a smile. 'I've had a fantasy about doing this,' he told Kate.

'What... taking off my glasses?'

'Mmm. And this.' Connor's hands went to the end of the braid hanging over her shoulder and he pulled off the band holding it together. He used his fingers to tease out the bends until her hair was completely loose. Then he wound lengths of it around his hands until they reached the back of her head and Kate couldn't move. He angled her head gently and bent his own to meet her lips with his.

And Kate still felt safe.

Floating in safety.

Free.

Her hands were on the back of Connor's head, urging him to deepen the kiss. Until he had to pull away.

'If I don't stop now, I won't be able to,' he warned.

'I don't want you to.' Kate was breathless. Panting, almost. 'I love you, Connor. I... I *want* you and I... don't want to wait. Please...'

Connor's eyes widened. He was genuinely shocked. 'I'm sure there's all sorts of rules about people carrying on like this in a hospital office space,' he murmured.

'I don't care,' Kate said. 'This is my office. I make the rules.'

Good grief.

This was Kate Graham. Breaking rules. Wild and wanton, just like that fantasy of unleashing the librarian he'd had about her in what seemed like a lifetime ago.

This was completely the wrong time and the wrong place, so why did it feel so right? So incredibly exciting all of a sudden?

Was it because Kate was free and this was her choice? The secrets of her locked-up past had been thrown into the open and they hadn't destroyed her. Instead, they seemed to have given her a new power.

Or was it because she felt safe with him? Safe enough to love him. Safe enough to agree to marry him. And she was safe. Connor had never felt so powerful. So confident that he could love and protect this woman for the rest of their lives.

And he was loving the way Kate was feverishly undoing his shirt buttons. The way she pressed her lips to the bare skin of his chest and then lifted her face for another kiss. Was he going to put the brakes on for the sake of rules made by people who couldn't possibly understand the miracle of what was happening here?

Not likely.

He cradled Kate close as he reached under the flaps of her white coat with its missing buttons to unzip her skirt. This was going to be the best sex she'd ever had, he could guarantee it. It would undoubtedly be the best he'd ever had because he'd never been in love with anyone like this before.

And maybe it was a bit frantic and a bit messy because they didn't even take off all their clothes and it wasn't very romantic even, but the cry of a woman's fulfilment had never sounded so sweet. His own had never been so heartfelt.

They could do romance later with candles and wine and soft sheets. They *would* do it later. Countless times, if he had any say in the matter. But nothing could beat this. A wild, triumphant leap into the future.

Their future.

* * *

MORE FROM ALISON ROBERTS

ABOUT THE AUTHOR

Alison Roberts is the author of over one hundred romance novels with Mills and Boon, and now writes romance and escapist fiction for Boldwood.

Download your exclusive bonus content from Alison Roberts here:

Visit Alison's website: www.alisonrobertsromance.com

Follow Alison on social media:

facebook.com/rosie.richards.75

x.com/RobertsAli54060

ALSO BY ALISON ROBERTS

A Year in France Series

Falling for Provence

From Provence, With Love

The Magic of Provence

A Wedding in Provence

Medical Romances

The Doctor's Promise

Doctor Off Limits

The Surgeon's Surprise Baby

A Kiss Before Midnight

Resisting the Surgeon

The Doctor's Second Chance

Stranded with the Surgeon

The Surgeon's Christmas Miracle

The Nurse's Second Chance

The Doctor's Guarded Heart

The Doctor's Chance at Forever

The Surgeon Who Stole Her Heart

Printed in Dunstable, United Kingdom

81795536R00102